RESCUING
PARK RANGER
BILLIE

CAROLINE COURT

Trafford rev. 07/31/2012

 www.trafford.com

North America & international
toll-free: 1 888 232 4444 (USA & Canada)
phone: 250 383 6864 ♦ fax: 812 355 4082

In Memory of Roy A. Lewis

CONTENTS

Season Three 2008

Season Four 2009

PROLOGUE

FIRESTARTER

Two a.m., no lights, no sound, except for a kitchen floor that creaks where joists underneath aren't just right, so I maneuver my way with care into the hallway toward our bedroom. The door is open. I stand still. No snoring. That means he could be awake, maybe not. I slink into the closet, drop my clothes and fumble around in the dark for a nightshirt. Skip the sink rituals, too much noise. For once I wish he were snoring; then I'd *know* he's asleep. I crawl into bed beside him on the new motion control mattress so a restless sleep doesn't keep the spouse awake, and I hope it works tonight. Now I'm lying in bed where I should have been hours ago.

"Billie," he whispers, but he doesn't need to whisper because I'm wide awake and so is he. "What happened?"

I hear a whine that worries me-maybe just wind. I prop myself on one elbow and think, *Of course he's awake. It's two in the morning and his wife just came home.* "Mum's in a semi-coma. There isn't much time left. You don't have to whisper." I feel like I'm buzzing, like sleep will not come tonight. I want to cry, but no energy.

He says, "I tried to call you on your cell, but you left it here. Were you with her all this time?" It is completely dark but my eyes are adjusting now.

There is that sad and distant drone like a train whistle. I fear it's a siren. *Someone saw me?*

"What's the matter, Billie?"

"That siren. It's getting louder. Oh, I hate alarms."

He leans toward me, "You're exhausted." *And I'm a desperado,* I think. "Do you want to sit up and have a glass of wine?" he asks.

I stiffen at the escalating volume of the emergency vehicle's siren, and I am sure it is for me and that I'm in a lot of trouble. My husband is watching my face in the dark. I can't see him but I feel his breathing quicken.

"Billie? What is it? Tell me."

"That siren is fading now."

I hesitate for another moment until there is just silence of the night, no siren, no police, and I feel safe. *Now I'll tell him.*

"Dr. Lanley said Mum isn't going to bounce back this time. I asked him about pain relief, palliative care, morphine. I thanked him, for ordering the morphine drip, I think. Then a nurse came. I was using her cell phone and she wanted it back. I handed it to her, thanked her too. All composed...then I lost it, couldn't look at anyone; I ran out of the room, down the hall. That alarmed the nurse so she rounded up a chaplain to talk to me. I was sobbing.

"I didn't call you because I left my cell somewhere, here I guess; I don't even know where, plus it was so late and I was crying. Anyway, the chaplain said, 'It happens to everyone.' I don't know what he meant. What happens? Everyone's mother dies? He was a chaplain. Aren't they professional about making people feel better? Well, I wasn't crying then at least, so I went back to Mum's room and sat with her and listened to her breathing. She was in a semi-coma the nurse said, but her lips were moving under her oxygen mask, chomping like her dentures were loose, but they weren't there. I thought she wanted her dentures. She wouldn't be caught dead without her teeth, you know. I knew they were back at the nursing home, so I went to get them."

Now he sits upright. "You drove over to the nursing home? In the middle of the night?"

"It was the only thing I could think of to do for her." I am exhausted but I've opened a floodgate and here it comes.

"It was way after midnight when I got to the home. I knew the code for entering the building. The code changes every few days. Getting in shouldn't be so easy, but . . . anyway, I took the elevator up to her floor. Three residents were hunched over their wheelchairs around a table in the dining room which is in full view of the nurse's station, looked like they'd been playing cards. One of them said. 'Hi, Billie.' He asked me how my mother was. He's one of the sweet ones. The two others were dozing in their chairs. I thought they should be in their rooms, in bed. There were no nurses at the nurses' station.

"You've been there; you know how the two hallways stretch from the nurses' station to dead ends so staff at the nurses' station can see everything in the hallways including call lights. There was a call light on at the end of Mum's hallway. But no staff. Usually doors to residents' rooms are open. If aides go into a room to care for a resident, they're supposed to close the door for resident privacy. Mum's door was closed. That seemed strange because Mum wasn't in the room, and her roommate was one of the three residents in the dining room.

"So I opened the door. A nurse's aide, a CNA, was in Mum's bed sleeping. Do you want to hear all of this?"

"Urgh," he clears his throat. "Damn it . . . but how could that . . . go on."

"And I forgot all about the dentures. Still no one at the nurses' station. There had to be an RN in the building somewhere. I wanted to report the sleeping CNA but who did I report her to? The phone was ringing at the nurses' station. It rang for a long time. Still no staff.

"I pulled the door shut and walked to the end of the hallway, to the room with the call light on. Myrtle, she's bedridden, was lying on her bed clutching a telephone, the old fashioned kind with a cord. I asked her if she needed help. She said her bed was wet and she had turned on her call light but no one came. So she called the nursing home to ask whoever answered to get some help for her on her wing." *The ringing phone.*

"Oh, Billie . . ."

"I'm not finished. I told the woman I would get help. I walked back to the vacated nurses' station, took a wastebasket off the floor and propped it on top of the nurse's desk, the one with the unanswered telephone. I searched in my purse until I found a matchbook and lit the loose papers in the basket. Then I picked up the phone, got an outside line and called 911. I said, 'There's a fire on the third floor of Riversite and no staff is here.' Then I hung up. The three people around the table were all dozing now, so they didn't see me or hear me when I said, 'Help is coming.'"

"Then you left?"

"Then I left and came straight here. Are you mad?"

My eyes have adjusted completely to the dark. I can see his face now. He doesn't look mad like when I got ticketed for speeding last week, but he's wide-eyed and his mouth is hanging open.

"You might have been arrested."

"I know. And the CNA wouldn't have been. I guess you see the irony. I hope you're on my side."

"The CNA, yes, dereliction of duty. But you started a fire. People get hurt in fires, Billie. What did you do *that* for?"

"I didn't hurt anyone," I insist.

Things have to add up for my retired accountant husband, so he begins his computations. "You'd just found out your mother is going to die soon, and then you go to her nursing home. You've been either baking chocolate chip cookies for staff there or setting up meetings with administrators over care issues for 6 plus years, and then you see a certified nursing assistant sleeping in Joan's bed and no other staff around. I think you probably wanted to burn down the whole place. But actually doing it? Why start a fire? If you wanted staff to come out of hiding, why didn't you just pull the fire alarm?"

"That didn't even occur to me. Maybe I didn't want to alarm the residents. There are already too many alarms going off."

"You could have called 911 without actually starting a fire."

"Then I would have been lying. I don't know. I don't know what I'm doing." And finally the tears come again, and I'm glad I'm not at the hospital with the chaplain who thinks this happens to everyone.

Now he puts both hands over his face and has thoughts he doesn't share with me—I think I'm grateful—before he begins again. "Okay, nobody got hurt. That's good," and he puts an arm around me and that feels better than good. "But now you can't report what you saw, no opportunity to register a complaint without incriminating yourself."

He pauses to think before he adds, "I had this picture of our golden years, retirement nest egg, becoming snowbirds, not hiring lawyers to defend my vigilante wife in a court of law, Billie." He gives me a firm squeeze; I think I'm forgiven.

Now he's out of bed and putting on his robe. He takes a deep breath, and I know he's made a decision or come to some kind of conclusion. "Billie, just one request, please. Actually two."

"Yes?"

"One, don't ever go back to the nursing home."

"Okay, I won't have any reason to anymore. What's two?"

"When this is over with, when Joan has gone and you have got your bearings, there's going to be a void . . . I mean, you spent a lot of time, daily, with Joan. What now?"

"I don't know. I thought she might be around for another 20 years, her number's up now. Maybe I'll sue Riversite during my new spare time."

He sighs, lets go of me and stands up. "I was thinking of something else, something healthful for you."

"Like you think I need a therapist?"

"I think you need a big distraction. Do you remember the one we talked about?"

"I'm not ready to move to Florida or anything major like that."

"No, not that. We used to take your mother to Fox Brook Park. She loved it. The two of you walked around the lake on the path. Then when she couldn't do the walking, you wheeled her in her chair and one day she saw a female park ranger there. That was magical for her, Billie."

"You want me, a woman in my fifties, to get a ranger job."

"Now, just think back. That job was *your* idea. Your mother got excited about *ranger*. She started to remember things, the old *Lone Ranger* television series, and we talked about the ranger's sidekick and what was his name and she remembered, *Tonto*. And you and I called out, 'Lone ranger awwwwaaaayyyy.' And then your mother corrected us.'"

"I do remember. It's a good memory." And it does make me smile.

"The horse was Old Silver, and your mother could remember all the details including the lone ranger calling out 'Old Silver away.' Except you'd be driving a Silverado pickup instead of Old Silver the horse."

"And nabbing garlic mustard from the woods instead of bandits from the plains."

"And working outside, meeting new people, beautiful distractions, Billie. Even your mother in her dementia saw the joy of it. Think about it?"

Analytical, rational, certified public accountant and good man. He's right although I'm not feeling the strength of reason now. Just desolation, loss. *It happens to everybody,* I remind myself.

"And, *Ranger Billie,* I'd like to have my wife back. You know, the one who used to smile, like this," and he takes his arms from around my shoulders, stands up, twirls like a ballerina, and forces his lips into a circus-comic grin. And I get another hug which I need before he flicks the switch on the wall. Now my eyes have to get used to light again. The kitchen floor is creaking, and I hear the cork pop out of the bottle. He's setting two glasses on the table, one for red and one for white, so I will drink my glass of Merlot and even though I can't think beyond the next 48 hours which is what the doctor says my mother has left in this world, I will say yes to what he asks.

SEASON ONE

2006

CHAPTER 1

DOG WHISPERER

Hauteur:
       *Arrogance,   conceit,
self-importance,   overconfidence:*
The Lexus driver. I call her the
haughty hottie of Fox Brook Park.
I'm sure she has a pet name for
me, too. Today she unloads her

royal cargo, elegant Salukis Nefertiti and Tutt (their real
names) and fails, as usual, to leash them, so the graceful and
unfettered canine siblings sniff around, snorting over spots
where lesser dogs have piddled or pooped before them.

I'm not impressed by the adolescent pink queen—she
snaps on pink rollerblades and wears a pink Packer visor—
or amused by her aristocratic dogs. Last week, she had

1

educated me. "First," she harped, "this may be the oldest known domesticated dog in history. They were *given* only as gifts or tributes to royals, not *sold*, and pharaoh owners in ancient Egypt mummified their Saluki pets." *Why am I supposed to care?* "In modern Islamic societies that consider dogs unclean, the Saluki is practically sacred, considered a gift from Allah."

She is full of herself and her holy dogs. Doesn't she know this is America and this is a public park? All dogs are created equal under the law. And I'm the law on this path. "Your dogs need to be leashed," I dictated then to the wheeled woman, and I'm doing it again now. She glowers, not in the least threatened by a park ranger uniform and the authority it confers. The skater with bling on her blades is dressed in the form fitting spandex favored by cyclists. Bootylicious and boobyluscious, she sizes up my working class Silverado pickup truck, masculine, boxy and dark green. Then her eyes move to my ranger uniform which could be described similarly with the addition of the modifiers polyester and machine washable, form fitting as a grocery sack. She assesses her situation and snarls, "I'm taking them for a swim."

"Be that as it may, they're not swimming right now." I'm going for pleasant but firm, seems an oxymoron at the moment.

But the young woman shakes the head that sits atop a slender neck, tossing lovely locks as though to cast off pollutants. I think how severe my tidy pony tail, pulled back tightly to accommodate a regulation ranger hat, must strike her, if anything strikes her at all. Then she tries to gather her dogs and leash them without losing her balance. Awkward but at the same time regal, the threesome lope and glide off to the west end of the lake where I know seven dogs in various states of "leashed" will have no respect for Tutt and Nefertiti's elevated station in dogdom.

Just a few minutes ago, I counted seven dogs at the west end of the lake, two in the water and the other five leashed. *Dogs must be controlled on a 6-ft. leash,* the signs say. But dog owners secure their pets when they see a ranger approach, not when they read a sign. How restrained they'll be in my absence is anyone's guess, so I expect a melee when two Salukis arrive.

And I will be called to sort out the dog debacle.

I could drive to the west end now, perhaps circumventing disaster for the Saluki tribe, but the value of a lesson learned through experience, rogue though that may be and not in the training manual, is best.

....

RANGER LOG

Date: **June 7**

Time: **3 p.m.**

Park foreman radioed for assist. Two unleashed Salukis encountered four other unleashed dogs at west end of lake; fracas followed. Park manager called by the city police who had been called by the Salukis' owner. Some difficulty on part

of dog owners gaining control of their dogs, combativeness on part of Saluki owner, but eventual compliance achieved and dogs leashed.

. . . .

Later, the beach crowd has thinned out considerably. By 7 p.m. only walkers and bikers remain and by sunset, desertion. Today has been dog people overload. My husband thinks this is good for me. I'm relieved to be seated in the truck's cab, facing west. Sunset—the best time to showcase the natural beauty of the park and the best place to be is at the east end of the lake facing west. The western sky glows in oranges and yellows or pinks and, I like to think, Merlot, which is what I might be sipping now if I were home tonight. The lake mirrors the sky, and as the sun sets, shadows elongate and fade. Box elder, oak and maple trees darken, and then it's over with. Day is done, dusk is here . . . *Someone on the beach is in silhouette, someone with a big, shepherd-like dog, someone throwing a ball into the water. The beach is closed for swimming—lifeguards gone for the day—and no animals are allowed on the beach anyway, plus swimming dogs have to go to the other end, the infamous west end, of the lake. Geez.* My dog day is not done.

I exit the Silverado and slam the driver's side door. The young man on the beach doesn't turn around at the sound. He's facing west, trying to signal his dog. *Waving at the dog?* The dog, tennis ball in its mouth, pops out of the water, appears to look for a command, then lunges toward the beach.

So far, I haven't been acknowledged by man or dog. "May I pet your dog?" A benign question, I think.

The man spins around now but only to pursue his dog who has lumbered up the beach to inspect me. Suddenly aware that he isn't the only person on the beach, the young man stops. Now he and I stand face to face, and I'm taken aback by his intelligent and blue, blue eyes, the eyes of the young Franco Nero in the movie musical *Camelot*, the eyes that Gwenevere fell in love with (and that the actress who played her fell in love with in real life) only set in a much younger but equally handsome face.

He wags his hand at the dog and makes a guttural noise that could not be called a word. The dog comes to heel next to the man. A trained dog!

Startled by the dog and still agape over the man's striking appearance, I blurt, "Your dog is welcome to swim in the lake but not in the beach area." I think I must sound tentative because he doesn't respond.

The man points to his mouth and opens his hand to suggest nothing there, emptiness. He indicates his inability to speak, facial expression of regret, lips turned down, and summons his dog off the beach. *A deaf-mute.* He is signing his dog and making limited utterances. *Wow, a dog that knows signing and must read lips, too.*

He retreats to a bench facing the lake, the dog seated next to the bench, watching the man, then watching me. Soon the deaf-mute begins again to sign to his dog. Fascinated with the dog whisperer aura and the bilingual capability of the young man, I begin to speak when suddenly he waves at me with one hand and with the other points to a woman careening awkwardly toward us on the bike path from the west. The man hails, with fluttering fingers, a breathless, gray-haired cyclist. She has that kind of dowager's hump that women with osteoporosis get, so maybe she's in her seventies? Still, she's hustling like a trooper to join the group as soon as she dismounts her bike and lets it collapse to the ground. "My son understands he's been told not to swim the dog at the beach. We would go to the west end but it's just too far for me to walk or bike. I've just been to the washroom and I'm already out of breath."

Okay, is this a moment for the ranger discretion that was discussed in training? No one is on the beach. Should I suspend the rules just this once? No, I explain the rules beginning with my oratory about creating a safe environment for families on the beach . . . which seems to be a cue for the mother to regale me with tales of her family and their solid good values and 17 grandchildren—she can hardly stop— and the wonder and miracle of her son and the dog, a mix-breed rescue, well behaved at only 9 months old, and on and on, and in fact, it all really is a wonder to me. Nobody is interested in swimming the dog now. *She wants me to know her family.*

So I join the refreshing threesome on the park bench, dog neatly tucked underneath, a violation at the beach. I explain the rationale for the rules, dogs capable of knocking over the many toddlers that wade in the water, dogs being out of control once unleashed, their owners leaving droppings that people then step on, etc.

She's attentive, actually listening. That is always appreciated by former teachers, so I go on. "The lake makes waterdogs of all—assorted labs, retrievers, setters, an occasional Irish wolfhound and bull mastiff, and the ubiquitous combinations of many breeds, plus the unusual Saluki. They all love the water.

"And there is not a single dog that or *who*, depending on your point of view, is bad. People are what they are and some of them are bad dog owners."

An awkward pause follows my angry rant. "Oh, I'm sorry. I guess I'm just venting."

The mother listens, respectful but probably not interested, and signs to her son who nods enthusiastically. Even the dog is polite, establishing eye contact with his master but maintaining a subservient presence.

The physically lopsided canine was a present to the young man, the mother explains. He didn't want a purebred lab or retriever though that's what a local organization supporting the handicapped offered. He wanted to rescue a dog. So during a visit to the Milwaukee Humane Society, he observed first the many dogs who sat at the front of their enclosures, anxious for the scent and presence of people. But one, described as anti-social and probably abused, sat as far away from the front of his pen as space allowed. "Abused" troubled the young man. He wanted to meet this one.

A caregiver approached the dog, cringing and whining in a corner.

"He trembled when he heard a man's voice, and he turned away when someone tried to touch him. We think

7

he'd been beaten with a hand or fist and who knows what else. Learning to trust, well, that was a big one for this dog. But he never had to cope with a man's voice again because my son hasn't got one."

I watch the two now, the young man and his motley dog. The tail's been shortened, a sort of botched docking, like someone just didn't like the tail and took an ax to it. One ear is erect, like a shepherd's, the other flops over like a lab's. But intelligence is there and so is trust. They are connected, more than that, *simpatico*; neither one can speak.

The mother addresses me, "I think they saved each other."

"Looks like a win-win to me," I add.

"That is so funny," she looks at my name tag, "Ranger Billie, that you said that," she laughs. "That's the dog's name! Winner."

Then she explains that the dog looks like a shepherd mix, black and brown, heavy in the shortened tail, not particularly elegant, but very smart. A dog DNA test supported her hunch that the dog had some lab, black lab, in his makeup.

"He's 75% lab," she announces, straightening her shoulders. Then she prattles on about her 17 grandchildren, but I'm still more interested in her son, how centered he seems. *He could be feeling sorry for himself. He could be mad at the world. Would I be? Am I?* Suddenly the mother stops talking.

"My son has a question for you. Are you the only ranger in the park?"

"Yes," I nod to him.

"Do you get scared in the dark he wants to know."

That's puzzling. The son is worried about me.

"No. But it is different. There is no lighting except for the light fixtures in the front parking lot. Everything becomes black, trees, lake; and nocturnal animals, coyotes, possum, raccoons are about so there are odd sounds. *Oh, but how does the mother sign 'sound' to a deaf mute?* I don't really like the darkness, but I am not scared by it. But to be honest, the only intense dark I like is coffee."

The son is pensive and thoughtful as his mother signs my answer. They both grin over the coffee.

Now she's on again about her 17 grandchildren, but I'm watching her son. *If he can't hear, he must compensate with vision. If it is very dark, he can't see or hear. In a park all he'd have left to save him is touch and smell. He'd be completely disabled in the park at night. Is that what he is thinking about?*

I interrupt the mother. "Is your son afraid of the dark? I read once that people who have lost both their vision and their hearing would choose, if given a choice, to have hearing restored. That kind of surprised me. I think I would miss sight more than sound."

The mother nods; she recognizes this sentiment. "You have never really heard silence, though, because you're a hearing person. There is always sound even in what you call silence. There is the *sound* of silence. The only true absence of sound is in a vacuum, like in outer space. But a deaf person knows silence. It's more isolating, more lonely, than darkness."

Now the dog suddenly stiffens, nostrils quivering as he catches the breeze from the west. One ear is up, one down. He has picked up the scent of other dogs. Rounding a turn in the bike path, they come into view.

"The Salukis are back," I think out loud.

"What beautiful animals," the mother observes.

They are not a delight to my eyes; I'm observing the absence of leash control and the distance between the dogs and their owner, the Queen of Sheba again. *Dogs must be on a 6-foot leash. Nefertiti and Tutt are attached to leashes but she isn't on the other end. They're dragging their leashes in the water.* "Can your son command his dog to jump into the lake?"

She signs the question to her son. His bright smile communicates the affirmative.

"Tell him to do it right now."

"But it's against the rules you said."

"I know. Go ahead and give the command."

Winner practically takes flight, then plunges into the swim area, paddling well beyond the deep water boundary but keeping his head up and watching for the next command. Meanwhile, elegant Tutt, Nefertiti and their owner have lost their cool.

"What should we do now?" asks the deaf-mute's mother.

"We should watch and enjoy." My unwholesome delight follows the decision to chuck the *discretion* referred to in my training manual. *What is discretion anyway? I think my ranger supervisor said it comes with experience. My mother said moderation in everything or is it discretion in everything?*

The Salukis' owner has taken off her rollerblades and entered the water. Inelegant now, she staggers, reaches, tips over; the dogs bark, splash, lunge . . . but after a complete soaking and considerable effort she is clutching the leashes and controlling her dogs. *Three stooges.*

"Now you can command your dog back," I say to the man who needs no interpreting from his mother. "Leash him and then you should probably be on your way. I feel an altercation coming."

I escort them to their car, not because they need escorting, just to defer the inevitable. Following their departure, I'll have words with queen of the Saluki tribe (and she with me) and the scene will be ugly.

. . . .

RANGER LOG

Date: **June 7**

Time: **9 p.m.**

. . . Dogs on beach. Altercation with owner of two Salukis. Lack of cooperation but eventual compliance achieved.

. . . .

The park has morphed into very black darkness, just as I said it would. The woman, her son and the dog had been respite after an afternoon that left me fatigued, disliking dogs and having dark thoughts about the people who ruined them. I recall the threesome's departure: Driver's side window rolling down, the woman calling out, "My son has a message for you." The son leaning over his mother, head out the window, dog head popped out the passenger window behind them. *Three smiling bobbleheads.*

"My son says for you to 'be safe' in the *dark park* tonight."

Just when I thought I'd never stop being mad at the world, just when I was sure dog people are trouble, a trio like that comes along to rattle my cage and move my cheese.

CHAPTER 2

MAN IN THE PANAMA HAT

One ranger duty—patrol the park. *The patrol.* Sounds like police work, but it's just public relations. Sometimes a minivan full of kids passes and the little ones inside scream *Daddy, it's a ranger, a ranger!* and wave to me.  Adoration. Openly adoring fans, refreshing for a former high school teacher. Sometimes a fisherman asks what kind of fish are in the lake, a stone quarry in its previous life. My response wows them: *croppie, bass, bluegill, perch and northern-watch out for snapping turtles . . .* Wowing fishermen is easier than wowing 15-17-year-olds in history class. Or a fisherman sees my uniform and nervously digs around his back pocket for his wallet, his fishing license, required at this suburban lake with urban rules, but the ranger's sheriff badge makes him think *police are after me,* so he is surprised when I lead him to where the big fish are biting and say, "Enjoy your day."

Sometimes park visitors bring nuisance animals into the park to release, like chipmunks and rabbits, gardeners' nemesis. Although not publically acknowledged, the practice is tolerated. The first time I came upon the old man in the Panama hat, he was eating his lunch at a picnic table near the point where turtles bask in the sun. At his feet, a no-kill trap, the kind that has a door at each end to contain, but not hurt, a captured small animal, sat empty. My intent wasn't investigation; I was on a public relations mission—the training manual: *Maintain a safe and enjoyable experience for park system guests.* I'd try for enjoyable since safety wasn't an issue, but I was approaching him from behind. *Better let him know I'm here.*

"I sure like your hat better than the one I'm wearing," I say.

Startled, he turns around. "Thanks. Have I broken some law?"

"Not that I know of."

But there is unease as he adds, "I was worried that someone had seen me release a chipmunk."

"I didn't see that. Actually, the foreman doesn't mind patrons bringing small animals in to release; he's more concerned about patrons trapping and taking animals out. Although you're welcome to take snapping turtles that you accidently snag when fishing."

But he's still defensive. "Some people think trapping and then releasing animals is bad. I wouldn't do it at all, but they're wrecking my wife's garden."

"Who thinks catching and releasing animals is bad?"

"The wildlife people on Wisconsin Public Radio. They say wild animals are territorial, and if you remove them from the territory they know, you are not helping them. Terrible things can happen to them in an unfamiliar environment."

"You mean they can't adapt?"

"They think the animals can't adapt. They starve or get killed by predators."

"Well, predators have to live, too. But go ahead with what you were telling me." So I sit down on the park bench and give the man my full attention.

"One of my neighbors used a kill-trap for his chipmunks after he listened to Milwaukee Public Radio. He had a snap trap, a big one, fit for a rat. I was with him in his back yard when he caught one he said he'd been trying to catch for a while. The trap caught the chipmunk on the back of its neck, but didn't kill it instantly. That thing thrashed, airborne at times, for about a minute. Then the neighbor said, 'It's over with.' Well, I stood over the trap and looked closer. The chipmunk had finished thrashing but its body was moving; it was still breathing!"

Agitated now, he challenges, "That was better than being released in this park? Maybe a coyote will eat a chipmunk that you release into the wild, but at least the chipmunk had a chance. And, like you said, the coyote needs to live, too. I'll go with nature."

"Hey, you don't have to convince me." *He's awfully worked up over a chipmunk.*

He looks away, then at his live trap, then, finally comfortable that I'm on his side, continues.

"I never liked killing animals, but my dad and my uncles expected me to hunt. I shot sparrows at first with a BB gun—never felt good about that. Then my uncles and Dad took me deer hunting. I killed my first deer. The custom was to cut out its heart, and that's what they expected me to do. I did."

He grimaces, "That was about the end of my killing animals."

I look away for a moment, indulging dark musings of my own, and consider sharing them with the man. Instead I just remark, "It's interesting what we remember, isn't it?"

"Uh huh. What about you? You like hunting?"

I sense a kindred spirit here. "I like being outside. My dad was a hunter. I had an older brother who died when he was 12. I was a year younger, and after he died I wanted a BB gun."

"Because he had one?"

"No, he wasn't even interested in hunting like my dad. Even so, I shot birds, blackbirds, *the bad birds*, according to Dad. My mother thought I was trying to cheer up my dad by behaving like a boy, an outdoorsy boy. But about a year later, I decided I liked animals in their alive state . . . I just wasn't a hunter or a boy. As a matter of fact, I was happiest when I had a bunch of animals to take care of.

"At one time," I expand to my rapt audience, "I had 18 assorted pets, not counting my tropical fish. Actually a whole menagerie. One dog, plus cats with kittens, a hamster, domestic rabbits and a few adopted bunnies and chipmunks and other wild life."

"So you never transitioned to deer hunting?"

"No, Dad set snares for rabbits in our yard; that was cruel. The harder the rabbit struggled to escape, the tighter the wire noose squeezed its neck. My dad said rabbits didn't feel much pain. I even asked my science teacher if that were true and all he could say was 'most amazing' which meant there really is such a thing as a dumb question. I used to set my alarm for 4 a.m., sneak out of the house, and pull the wire nooses, close them so they couldn't snare a rabbit, then go back to bed. My dad said the rabbits were developing intelligence and had figured out a way to close those nooses. 'Most amazing,' I said, and never told him I did it. Subterfuge became part of my character. Anyway, I don't like killing animals either."

The formerly tentative man is smiling now. "Did your dad stop snaring rabbits then?"

"Yes, he stopped then. And about 40 years later, just before he died, he told my mother he felt bad about snaring those rabbits. Probably not out of empathy for the rabbits, though. Maybe he feared a rabbit would greet him at the Pearly Gates. Or maybe guilt. I don't know. It took him a whole lifetime, but he eventually came around. I think we're all works in progress."

He's looking over the water now, maybe looking into his past. "My father and his brothers kept hunting."

"They probably thought they were molding you into a man. Something in Wisconsin hunter culture. You kill a large animal and you've crossed over, into manhood. I guess you did cross over, too, because at that moment you decided you weren't doing the killing thing anymore."

But the man doesn't look convinced. He pauses, perhaps considering his choices: let a painful memory surface or keep it repressed. "I did service in Viet Nam. No one in the Cato family can say no to service. My uncles drilled that into my head. I was drafted. And I saw combat. It's nothing but destruction . . . war . . . We weren't put on this earth to destroy. That's why God made Jesus a carpenter, don't you think?" he asks but just continues. "Construction, building up. That's what we're supposed to be about. So when I came back, I marched with war protesters, Vets against the war.

"Yup. My uncles' plans backfired. A work in progress. Yeah, I've done all right. At least I know who I am now. And you! You liked the outdoors and wild life and now look where you are." He gazes admiringly around the park. "You've done well for yourself," he beams.

I'm not doing all right, though. That's why I'm here. To get myself right again. Meanwhile, I put on my ranger hat and say, "I have to get back to patrolling the lake. I'm supposed to help park patrons have an enjoyable experience. How am I doing?"

"I did not expect to have such an enjoyable time at the park today!" he declares.

"And now your wife has one less chipmunk digging up her garden. Does she know you bring them here?"

He hesitates. "Umm, it's hard to know what she knows. She's in a nursing home now. I take care of her garden. I used to take her back to the house and she liked to sit and watch her garden, but now that's pretty hard because walking is so hard for her. I take her home whenever I can get someone to help me get her in and out of the car."

"She had a stroke?"

"She's got Alzheimer's."

"Which nursing home?"

"Riversite."

That information gives me pause, no more questions.

"Well, I'm glad you can come here and enjoy the park," I deflect. "Bring your chipmunk buddies any time. If you'd like to bring your wife sometime, she might enjoy herself, just sitting in the car, facing the lake." *Like my mother did.* "A ranger could help you get her out of the car and into a wheelchair. Then you could wheel her around the lake; it is wheelchair accessible."

He doesn't respond but he smiles, picks up his trap and waves.

. . . .

RANGER LOG

Date: *July 9*

Time: *11 a.m.*

Engaged elderly gentleman having lunch at north end of lake, encouraged him to return with . . . disabled wife to . . . make use of wheelchair accessible path around lake.

. . . .

I didn't tell the man in the Panama hat that my mother had been in the same nursing home as his wife, that she had Alzheimer's and that I used to bring her to the park and wheel her around the lake, or that she died. And I don't know why I didn't tell him because I didn't have any trouble telling him about the rabbits.

CHAPTER 3

BOG BIKE

. . . .

BROOKFIELD NEWS POLICE BLOG

June 25

Collision: Female pedestrian alleges male cyclist traveling west on Mitchell Park's boardwalk knocked her into the Brookfield wetlands at approximately 10 a.m., June 20. Cyclist did not stop. Pedestrian, a Brookfield resident, was examined by paramedics and released.

. . . .

That is the story according to the police report as it appeared in the Brookfield News police blog. It is what happened, but it's not all of  what happened. If the truth were told, from the point of view of the Brookfield resident, the one struck by the bike, it would go something like this . . .

It's a sunny June morning around 10 a.m., and I'm on the boardwalk ruminating about the state of the world, my world, about the six years advocating for better care at my mother's nursing home, about getting a part time job as a 57-year-old park ranger after she died, just so I wouldn't spend so much time ruminating . . . and being angry about the state of affairs for the elderly in America. Anyway, I got myself pretty worked up and embroiled in Walter Mitty fantasies about ridding the world of nursing home neglect and abuse when out of nowhere a bike slams into me from behind.

My left foot is mid stride, so I spin on my right foot, twisting the ankle, becoming airborne, and landing on ground beneath the boardwalk. The back of my head hits first, energy of impact rippling through me like a snapped towel, crack of head, then hip, then tailbone on hard, crenellated ground, the cement-like floor of a rain deprived wetland. I am conscious but can't move or speak. There's no pain, just a dull numbness and strange awareness of breathing; *I must be alive because I'm breathing.* I'm not sure, though. Then I see the form of a man above approaching on my right, on the boardwalk; he's jogging with a black, shepherd-like dog at heel. It's the deaf mute and his perfectly trained dog. *Can't they see me? Am I even really here?* The dog turns its head, takes in my scent, but the man and dog continue past; the man doesn't see me, flat on the ground amidst tall grasses, and I'm momentarily mute myself. *Why couldn't the dog have been out-of-control like so many at the park? One who would bolt for me now. Maybe I am dead, not here or almost dead or in a state of shock, profound shock like on the television show* Wild America. *The downed animal, in shock, doesn't feel anything, the narrator said, not as brutal as it looks.* I never believed that, but here I am, knocked off my feet, paralyzed and feeling no pain.

Eventually—I'm not sure if seconds or minutes elapse—I am able to raise myself up on one elbow so my eyes are level with the boardwalk. To my right about 30 yards away, a cyclist is straddling his bike and looking back over his shoulder. I try to speak, but still cannot. I am sure he is looking directly at me. But he rights his bike and begins peddling away. *He sees me . . . he's not going to stop.* My reaction is disbelief, I want to scream, *I am not road kill!* But I cannot yet vocalize my rage.

I hear sounds of running on the boardwalk, the vibrating planks. Paramedics are alongside; someone has seen me and called 911. A cuff is around my arm. "Your blood pressure is in high normal range, 148/90, no lacerations," the paramedic reports. A police officer arrives.

"She is able to walk, no fractures," the paramedic reports to the officer. The paramedic says to me, "This is your lucky day. You should buy a lottery ticket." Sensation has returned, but I don't feel lucky.

Officer Smithson, tall, lean and all business, asks for a description of the bike and biker. All I recall is he was heading west toward Fox Brook Park, a young man, maybe college age, and maybe the bike was red, even that is fuzzy. No other details.

"Did he actually hit you or did you lose your balance being startled by someone coming from behind?"

"Something actually hit me, from behind. A bicycle." My hip is sore, my ankle is too, from twisting. The paramedic says I'll have bruises, but an emergency room visit isn't necessary. The policeman offers me a ride home.

"No, I'm on my way to the park, I'm a ranger there . . . Do you think he'll come back?"

"Not likely. They don't return to the scene of the crime. Whoever he is, he knows he hit you. It's broad daylight. He couldn't have missed seeing you. Hit and run."

"How could he just not stop?"

"Could have been drunk. Could have had a record. Could have panicked. Sometimes they turn themselves in later. I'm talking about automobile hit and runs. Don't get many bike hit and runs. I'll walk with you to Fox Brook. You may change your mind about going to work."

But my focus is completely on the cyclist. "He was headed toward Fox Brook Park. Shouldn't we look there for the bike?"

"We? I'll handle this. Don't you go looking for this guy." He is firm on that point. "That's our job."

Leave it to the professionals, heard that before. Advice people gave me when Mum was in the nursing home.

So he escorts me to Fox Brook Park; I guide him to the bike rack and watch as he identifies red ones which may match what I think I saw. There are at least five male red or burgundy bikes, several black, one silver and white. None is damaged, and I admit to myself, I am not entirely sure the bike I saw is one of these.

Next we enter the concession area, and I scan the green slope where boys and young men sunbathe and situate themselves to ogle bikini clad girls who cluster beneath the embankment on the adjacent beach. A teenage boy is buried in the sand, except for his head. His buddies have built a giant sand penis above what would be his groin if it weren't covered in sand. I admonish the boys in a tone practiced as a high school teacher and reinvented here for my ranger voice, "This is a family friendly beach." The boys howl and knock over the sand phalanx.

"There is police work in my job, too, Officer Smithson."

"I see what you mean." He grins, finally.

"I was squinting into the sun when I saw the biker facing my direction. I can't recall any detail of his face. He could be any of these young guys here." I'm looking west now, into the sun, peering, trying to remember more than just a silhouette.

"Are you sure you're ready to go to work? That was a hard fall you took."

"Yes, I'm sure. I don't want to go home. I'm better off staying busy here, so I'm going to go to the office and change into my uniform. Thanks for your help."

"I'll let you know if anything develops. One of our detectives may call you."

. . . .

I don't wait for the police department to perform any miracles, though. Still smarting from the lack of skill in *skilled* nursing care and the lack of care in nursing *care*, my cynicism regarding professionals has leeched into my perception of *professionals* in all bureaucracies, including law enforcement, so the next day, I return to the scene and watch cyclists on the recreational boardwalk. It spans about a mile of wetland, connecting Brookfield's Mitchell Park with its picnic grounds and dog run to Waukesha County's Fox Brook Park, with its beach and lake. The boardwalk is for convenience for pedestrians and cyclists and protection from motor vehicles. But it doesn't protect pedestrians from cyclists like the one who plowed into me.

Recreational bikers approach now. They ride cruisers with little bells ringing. This is a family group now, taking it slow so three little kids can keep up. They carefully and courteously negotiate passage past me and the dog walkers ahead of me. Now I'm thinking, ruminating again, about the serious bikers, the ones in training for races—the most dangerous for pedestrians. They bike for a workout and that means fast. They don't always have patience for the courtesy "left" warning as they approach from behind. Those bikes become dangerous projectiles careening around and through pedestrian traffic on a boardwalk with no railings; falls can happen, easily. *Maybe the biker who hit me has a routine.* So I make my personal pilgrimage for several consecutive days, decide that's too time consuming and obsessive and instead resume just on Saturdays and Sundays since my assailant appeared on a previous Sunday. My hunch, unlike Officer Smithson's, is he will return to the scene of the crime.

. . . .

In July, one sunny but humid Sunday, I stop near the boardwalk bridge over a tributary of the Fox River. Children are enticing ducks and geese with little pieces of their sandwiches, children and fowl enjoying the wetland which is lush now, the water almost level with the boardwalk. A biker has stopped his cycling on the west side of the bridge. He's wiping his forehead and squinting into the wooded western edge of the bog. A deer sighting. The way he's straddling his bike; it's familiar. A silhouette I've seen before. *It's the posture, an exact replica of what I saw from the hard bottom of the bog floor earlier this summer. The bike is maroon, not red, but it's him.*

I know Officer Smithson would forbid this, my stalking someone, and my heart is thumping away. I'm headed west, toward Fox Brook, like the biker that day. I pass him, keep walking, and feel my respiration increase. *He won't stay at the bridge forever.* I listen carefully for his approach. *He's going to be passing me.* When he is near, I anticipate his "left," but it doesn't come, just like last time. Then he's passing me. This time I've got a good look at the details of the bike. It's a Micargi Road Racer. I follow him to Fox Brook, and to do that I pick up my leisurely pace; I'm jogging, running and nearly out of breath when he parks his bike, locks it with a bike cable, and carries his beach pack into the concessions building. The hot day is the kind that swimmers love, the kind that can dehydrate cycling enthusiasts. This cyclist is probably there to settle in for an afternoon on the green embankment of hormone-charged adolescents.

Fox Brook's park office garage is open; a small toolbox, the defibrillator I hope never to need, and the 4-gallon pail for picnic debris not properly disposed of are ready for my use. I select the item I'll need for my task, drop it in the front pocket of my cargo shorts and proceed to the office but don't punch in or put on my uniform.

By late afternoon the beach area is populated mainly with teenagers and college kids. Young mothers with toddlers begin to leave after the midafternoon beach drill which is usually 3 p.m. to 3:20 p.m. Everyone has to come out of the water while the guards do safety drills. Many visitors just call it a day.

The cyclist is approaching the bike parking area where he left his Micargi and he looks puzzled. His bike is gone. I'm standing about four feet away, watching. He asks me if I saw someone take his bike. He doesn't recognize me from earlier on the boardwalk. He saw me from behind then.

"A lot of people have left on bikes this afternoon. Was yours locked?"

"It was cabled."

"Didn't I see you earlier today on the boardwalk? I think you stopped at the bridge. You were looking at a doe in the tall grass."

"Yeah, I was there. You saw my bike, then."

"Yes, and I saw you again when you passed me without warning, no 'left' signal."

He's thinking now but not speaking.

I continue, "Do you remember passing someone on the left and not signaling?"

"No." He's having no trouble with eye contact. I'd say he's glaring at me, and I'm thinking how enthralling a sting operation can feel.

"I believe you passed me near the spot where a cyclist collided with a woman and knocked her down earlier this summer. You know that spot? You do know, don't you?"

"I'm calling the police."

"Good. Ask for Officer Smithson . . . I think he's familiar with that case."

"Why do you keep bringing up *that case*? I'm looking for my bike."

"There's a lot of bike traffic here. If it's been here all afternoon and it wasn't secured . . ."

"It was locked."

I'm a ranger, but I'm un-uniformed right now. Still, the pedagogue in me comes out and I tell him what to do.

"Go to the park office. The foreman will write a report on the missing bike."

After he is out of sight, I picture the foreman calling the police, reporting the incident, the kid describing his bike. Then the kid comes out of the building and heads back to the boardwalk on foot. I tell myself I'm not stalking him; I'm following him, observing, watching with vigilante relish as he peers beyond the Fox River over the patch of bog where I myself had lain weeks ago.

He recognizes one wheel of his upended, submerged maroon $380 Micargi peeking out of muddy water. I'm smiling, even thinking of waving to him, but decide not and just put my right hand in my pocket. The other hand is fondling the cut cable that's in my left pocket.

Satisfied now that my act of subterfuge is complete, I turn and walk lightly, back to the park, where I will put on my uniform, punch in, make some excuse for not having done so earlier, and later in the afternoon, the foreman will probably inform me that the missing bike has been found.

. . . .

But two weeks later, the park foreman calls me on his radio. "Officer Smithson is here to see you. Your supervisor is here, too."

Uh-oh. Did someone see me pedal away on the Micargi? I didn't have my uniform on; I certainly didn't stand out. No one was on the boardwalk when I disabled the bike and pushed it into the water. But, geez, this is a bad sign.

I climb into the Silverado and drive past the beach toward the office. My view: The foreman standing outside engaged in conversation with two adults, a man and woman, neither of whom I recognize and both glancing nervously in my direction; a crying teenage boy; and Officer Smithson in his lean, mean and non-smiling mode leaning against his squad car. My supervisor is apart from them. He's sitting in his sheriff's deputy car. I can't tell what he's thinking, no expression on his face.

I park my vehicle next to Officer Smithson who says nothing. Two grim adults approach, their boy boxed between them. I emerge from the cab of the Silverado. *I already feel guilty and I don't know for which of my transgressions I'm about to be condemned.*

Through sobs, and with his father griping his left arm and his mother the other, the teenager blubbers, "I'm the one who hit you. I'm so sorry. I thought I would get into trouble. And I did. Cause it wasn't my bike I was riding. I took it, but I would have taken it back. But I'm really sorry and I'm glad you're okay."

The father says his son tweeted a confession to a friend, that he stole a bike and knocked someone off the boardwalk. The word got around as secrets do when you tell them to anyone; the parents confronted their son, told him he would have to confess and apologize.

Now the boy is scared, the tears are real. I'm scared, too, but somehow manage to channel the fear into questions. "Why did you change your mind that day, I mean about stopping and helping me? I mean you did stop. You must have been thinking about it."

"No. I never stopped. I just pedaled faster," between sobs.

"But, I . . . thought I saw you look behind . . . at me."

"No, I just kept going, but faster."

"What color was your . . . the bike?"

"Silver and white."

Geez . . .

Now I take charge, and with a nod to Officer Smithson, offer, "Well, I accept your apology, and I don't plan to press charges of any kind. You're lucky to have such good parents, teaching you the value of social responsibility."

The irony . . .

It wasn't a silver and white bike I saw. And I did see a man and he did stop. Someone who was on the boardwalk . . . some time elapsed . . . I don't know how much . . . maybe after the silver and white bike, a second bike, maybe maroon . . . passed me, someone who didn't see me, like the man jogging with the dog didn't see me. I got the wrong guy? . . . Oh well, Saddam didn't have weapons of mass destruction after all, but the world is better off without him, right? Isn't that what our president said?

Well, he was rationalizing then and I am now. Still, the boardwalk is better off minus one reckless rider and his racing bike. Especially since said rider didn't signal an approach. One less discourteous and errant rider.

32

. . . .

There is one person with a little larceny of spirit, some unresolved anger issues, and lots of cynicism, one rogue ranger who knows the real story the police blog didn't completely tell, of how a bike  got into the bog. And that's the way it will be until the Pope converts to Islam or I confess, whichever comes first.

CHAPTER 4

FIRST MEETING WITH THE SUP

. . . .

RANGER BILLIE'S JOURNAL

July 17

. . . .

My supervisor is coming to the park tonight, and he's probably going to assess how I'm doing as a first season park

ranger. I have had a few mishaps that he doesn't know about—might tell him, though. But not everything.

One responsibility I have is locking up the shelters when the park closes. The park is pitch black at night; I think I didn't know how dark the dark can be until this park at night. And when I lock up the shelters, I also have to turn off the lights, plus set the alarm. Once the alarm is activated, I have 10 seconds to get out of the building or motion sensors will set off an ear bursting siren, plus a county deputy is automatically called to the "break-in." If the alarm activates, I have to call the park manager, the sheriff's department and the alarm company, and the blast is so loud, I am sure I wouldn't be able to even hear the phone conversation. A false alarm can be embarrassing plus noisy, so I want my first attempt to be flawless.

I know the sequence of numbers to punch in—the park foreman showed me once during orientation in the park office building, but I hadn't set it in the main shelter, so I radio my sup who is patrolling the other parks and ask him if he wouldn't mind coming out to go through it with me. He says he's tied up in another park, he's never set the alarms at Fox Brook, and his advice would be *get it right the first time.*

Whoa.

First, I unlock the front door (locked previously by the departing lifeguards) of the main building to let myself in. I check the utility room, the concessions area, the lifeguard's room, and the woman's bathroom. Everything seems to be in order, so I start locking doors. I go to the utility room where the "box" for setting the alarm is located. I don't know where the light switch is so I pull out my flashlight and it doesn't work. *Damn it.* Then I go back to the truck to get another flashlight out of my first aid kit. Back inside I go over the code and very carefully punch in the numbers. There is a click which indicates the countdown has begun. *Oh damn it again.* I remember I haven't checked the men's bathroom. I dash in and realize I have turned out the lights and there is no light in the cavernous bathroom which also encloses showers, and as I'm fumbling along the wall, I bump into multiple doors.

What flashes before my eyes now is the image of a news story, really dark thoughts, a guy who was falsely imprisoned, then released, then returned to his junkyard livelihood. A woman, alone, knocked on the door of his trailer. The pervert, with the help of his nephew, raped and then stabbed her to death and stuffed her into a trash can and burned her dismembered body. *Don't think about stuff like that now! Where's the damn exit door? And how many seconds are left?*

Then there's the news story about the mother who let her 9-year-old son go to the bathroom in a California state park at 11 p.m.—alone. A pervert in there sliced his throat. *Where's the damn door!*

I have my flashlight and it works, good thing, but I open a broom closet door, a utility room door and an inside lodge door before I finally get the hell out without being raped or murdered, without activating the alarm but not without increasing my gray hair count. Someday I'll tell the other rangers I got lost in the men's bathroom but not yet. I wonder if I should tell this to my sup. Only if he asks me.

The sup did not come tonight. Phew. No confessions. Maybe he'll come tomorrow.

. . . .

July 18

. . . .

A man is fishing off the paddleboat pier—another park no-no.

I approach him, introduce myself as per the manual, *Hello, I'm Ranger Billie of the Waukesha County Parks. How are the fish biting?* Dumb question because I am working up to telling him he can't fish there. He says there are some big fish in this spot. So I tell him I am sorry but he can't fish off the pier—*as the sign clearly says*, I think.

So he moves to the north, to the paddleboat beach. But he isn't supposed to fish there, either, which I try to diplomatically point out, but I think it's too late for diplomacy.

"Why not?" he asks.

"Because tackle sometimes come lose and we have concerns about kids' bare feet coming into contact with hooks." His smile has a crooked edge to it.

He says, "Where are the kids?"

I guess he doesn't care about rules or kids' feet.

I say, "It's my job to tell you about the rules. You can fish in the lake but not at the beach or from this pier"

"You mean I paid good money to come in here and fish in a public place and I can't fish where I want?"

"Actually, the fee you paid is for parking your car here. I am not trying to hassle you."

"Yes you are."

"You just need to move to a different location."

"Are you going to arrest me?" *Ohhhh, hostile, and I would so much like to have handled this successfully.*

"No, but I may have to ask you to leave the park if you are unwilling to cooperate." I don't even talk this way in my real life. It's the training manual. In real life I'd be thinking either a contrite *I'm sorry* if I were trying to save my life or a belligerent *it's my way or the highway, so cut the crap* if I had backup.

At that point I move away from him, back to my truck. The manual says to always let the park patron save face and to diffuse confrontational situations. I think if I get out of his face, he'll save face, maybe take his face and move it to a different location. He doesn't.

Training phrases flash before me: *Avoid conflict . . . studied response vs. a natural reaction . . . deflect and redirect . . . stand tall . . . blah, blah.*

On my first full day of rangering, I was mentored by a veteran who told me she had been a Native American in a previous life. I had no reason not to believe her; I wasn't there. Anyway, the key to rangering well, she told me, was "the walk." Walk like you're part of the earth. Walk like you and the earth are one. The Native Americans can do it with their eyes closed she told me. It worked for her; she looked natural, commanding but benign at the same time. I tried the earth walk, but my gait seemed awkward, waddle-like.

So at this moment I decide to take my mother's advice (stand up straight) and my ranger manual's instruction (stand tall) and hope the park patron will cooperate (stand down).

I walk down the hill standing tall and hoping he isn't packing heat. Just before I get to him, he bends over and reaches for something. *Uh—oh.* He picks up fishing gear and moves away.

He mutters something about what a good job I am doing. *I think the "F" word might have been among his comments.*

Then my supervisor came and I told my story.

First he told me because of my education, my bachelors degree, masters degree, and the fact that I'd been a teacher for 33 years, he expected me to be intelligent. *Ouch.* I think he first suspected *studid* when I struggled with my two-way radio. When I finish a shift, I'm supposed to call in, "935 to 930, requesting 10-42." That translates to, "Ranger Supervisor, this is Ranger Billie at Fox Brook requesting permission to call it a night and leave now." The ranger who trained me, the former Native American, was fond of my botched attempts to get the codes right. She said I amused her.

Not amused, my sup said," You don't have to take crap, and you could just call me and I would make sure the guy was taken care of. You're not a policeman. What did I tell you in training?"

"To try to solve my problems myself. If I can't, then I should call a deputy for help. But the guy did comply and I'll save you for when I can't get compliance. I think that's using discretion."

What's behind the blank expression? It was like a mask. I couldn't get a bead on his assessment of me. Maybe that blank mask served him well when he was active in law enforcement. He had to deal with criminals. *Like a woman who lights a fire in a nursing home?* Is he a nice guy who learned to act tough, or is he a tough guy who has to work on being nice? He wanted to know how I really feel about this job. "You have an answer for everything. What about this job? Do you like it?"

I wasn't sure how to answer that question, partly because I honestly didn't know yet. "Sometimes I like it a lot. It's a beautiful place to spend a day or evening shift three or four times a week. Sometimes I don't like it so much. Isn't that how most people feel about their jobs?"

"Go on."

"I hate being nice to assholes." Right after I said that, I wished I'd used more appropriate language, but he didn't blink.

"You mean the Saluki owner?"

"That's a good example."

"Why didn't you get the name of the Salukis' owner?"

Rangers are supposed to be good witnesses, get names and other details for reports.

"I did get her name. I just don't remember it right now."

He didn't like that. Here I am being evaluated, and I say *I just don't remember.* I didn't like it either, the fact that I didn't remember. I remembered the nickname I gave her, though.

"I call her Sheba, queen of the SS. I don't know her real name because I don't want to know her because I don't want to waste my memory on such a—I started to say bitch—bad person as she, and now I'm probably going to get fired . . . that would be no big deal to me. I don't need the job for financial reasons; it's just a distraction for me." I didn't know what I was so mad about. It just came out like that. Now I think maybe Sheba annoyed me because of her unearned status or maybe because of her psychological armor; she probably never suffers, and I was suffering, wallowing a bit in self pity. But the self pity came out anger.

The sup's expression never changed. "And are you going to tell me what you need to be distracted from?"

"Yes, I need a distraction from my own dark thoughts, and that's the truth. It's such a long story." And I didn't want to go there.

He didn't look impressed; actually he didn't look anything. He waits but he doesn't demand. Maybe he's a man with dark thoughts of his own. Finally, after watching two patrons drive out of the park and slow down when they saw his marked squad car, he said, "Thirty-three years teaching high school kids, and a woman with two frilly dogs gets under your skin? What's wrong with this picture?"

I felt inadequate then and I said so.

Maybe that's what he wanted to hear, some insecurity and a little groveling, a nod to his authority. Even so, he came to my rescue, "Venting is good. We all need to decompress. But here's what I need to know. Are you going to stick it out? I mean I can respect that you might not come back next season if isn't what you expected . . . But if you quit mid season?"

The tone was chilly, not sympathetic. His question was a challenge.

"I am not a quitter." And that is true and the second thing he wanted to hear because then he actually smiled.

"You're doing well for a rookie." Evaluation complete. I passed.

But he doesn't know about the bog bike; he doesn't know my contribution to the Saluki incident, either, about how I escalated instead of de-escalated the situation. He doesn't know that I'm not entirely law-abiding, too. That's okay. That's okay for today. And that's all for today which in ranger language is 10-42.

CHAPTER 5

FALLING FROM BALLOONS

Perfect day at Fox Brook. Sunny, a few billowy clouds, low humidity. Hot, humid weather brings out beach fans; bus loads of kids on day camp trips converge on the sand. More people, more problems. Kids don't want to get out of the water, but life guards have to clear the swim area to do their safety drills in the water at 1, 3, and 5 p.m. The ranger helps

by patrolling the beach and corralling errant children,

toddlers who wander into the water when their sometimes inattentive parents don't see them.

Then there are the teenagers. Teenagers drinking questionable beverages in their insulated cups. Can't have glass on the beach. Some groups bringing in cases of beer in spite of signs: "No alcohol in the park." *But if people read signs, no rangers would have jobs.*

Fewer people at the park, generally fewer problems, and today is cool, less attractive to swarms of beachgoers, more appealing to hikers, dog walkers, fishermen and picnickers. And apparently for an outing with a disabled individual. A man on the bike path is pushing a wheelchair. I spy him in silhouette, the familiar Panama hat.

A hot and humid day would be hard on the man's wife.

Mum . . . overheated but didn't think to take off her sweater. Might be dehydrated but didn't think to drink the water that was right in front of her. Could feel uncomfortable, maybe needed to be toileted, but couldn't articulate . . . so many memories. "Those dark thoughts," I mutter to myself.

. . . .

My paperwork today designates a private party reservation, with beer permit, at the north shelter. I'm about 10 feet away from a brawny, shirtless teenager who's hauling a half barrel into fireplace enclosure of the north picnic shelter. Permit-carrying patrons can consume beer, "malt beverages" and wine coolers, but not wine—these rules are hard to explain to patrons. A middle-aged woman, part of this family reunion gathering has set out a few opened bottles of red wine. It's time for ranger discretion. I quote the wine prohibition rule from my manual and add, "Don't open any more bottles, please." The woman doesn't argue. She's redfaced from embarrassment, not belligerence. That's refreshing. Then she places the bottles under a table between bags of potato chips. Seeing no trouble developing here, I shift my focus to the man in the straw hat and his companion.

They have reached the north end parking lot near the picnic pavilion, and he's trying to get her back into his car. I shift from stroll to jog, arriving in time to offer assistance.

"Here I am. Are you a taxpayer? If so, I am at your service."

Beads of perspiration on his old forehead, he is in no frame of mind to refuse help. "I decided to take you up on your suggestion, Ranger Billie. The park foreman helped me get her out. Now I need help getting her back in."

I squat in front of the woman. "Welcome to Fox Brook Park. I'm Ranger Billie." We're eye level now and I'm smiling. She smiles back but doesn't speak.

"I'm going to help you out of your chair and into the car. Your husband is going to take you home then."

"Yes, I want to go home," she says.

The man adds, "She always wants to go home."

A collapsible transport chair (like a wheelchair only small rear wheels) is dangerous if the wheels aren't locked.

Stirrups are a tripping hazard, too, as the rider isn't always aware they are even there.

"Why don't you open the passenger door of your vehicle and I'll handle the rest," I say to the man as I lock the wheels and remove the stirrups. "Can she walk at all?"

"With a walker, barely, but pretty unsteady."

"Okay, I'll lift her out."

I bend over in front of the woman, wrap my arms around her waist, lift her out of the chair in one motion, turn toward the car, set her on the seat in a second motion, and then gather her feet and legs under the dashboard.

"Voila!"

"You've done that before. Is it part of ranger training?"

"No. They didn't train me. Let's just say I'm self taught."

"Well, thank you so much. You made it look easy. What a gorgeous day to be alive," the man says to the sky, to the few wispy clouds. Then to me, "Did you ever see balloons up there?"

"You mean balloons like in *Around the World in 80 Days*?"

"Yes, with the passenger baskets?"

"I've seen them in the area. Never directly over this lake, though. Why do you ask?"

"I dreamed of one last night. I wonder why I did."

"Good dream or bad?"

"I think pretty bad, but I'm not sure," he says as he looks at his wife. She doesn't return his gaze.

"Tell me about it; I'll give it my official ranger interpretation."

He looks again at the sky, squinting as he recalls, "I dreamed I was in a rural area, like this park, something about a dog like a labradoodle running around fetching things, puppy behavior and a guy who said his mother trained dogs professionally. He said he could train this dog—don't know if it was mine, but I told him I wasn't looking to hire someone to train the dog. He said he could do a lot of training in just one hour and then he would bring the dog back. He was leaving by balloon to go to where he lived with his wife. So I said it was okay to take the dog for an hour. Then he left in the balloon with the dog. I watched the balloon go up into the air."

"So far it's not a nightmare. Just dog and balloon."

"Then to my horror, I thought I saw something hanging out of the basket, and then it kept falling. It was the dog. It fell and fell to earth. I was mortified."

"Now it's a nightmare." I'm thinking *Tales from the Crypt*.

"I had given the dog over and it had been killed."

I'm watching the woman in the car as he tells his story, but I'm thinking about my own bad dreams. Now no one is talking. The silence makes the man uncomfortable, embarrassed.

"It was just a dream. I don't know what it means."

I'm focused now on the wife, her arms, the bruises.

"Is your wife having falls?"

"Why, yes, she had a fall."

"Just one fall?"

"One that I know of."

"One that the nursing home told you about. It happened on a weekend?"

"Yes. You know that?"

"So you put your wife in a home, now she's falling, you can't do anything except trust her to the professionals, they're not stopping her falls, you feel helpless to protect her, you feel guilty and it's playing out in your dreams."

I'm looking right into his eyes. He doesn't blink. His face reddens, jaw tightens and those grey-blue eyes tear up. Then he looks away.

I check myself, not because I don't have plenty more to say on the subject, but because he doesn't need some ranger stranger making him feel worse, and it's none of my business anyway. *I wish I would have just shut up.* But now I want to repair the damage. "You're hard on yourself. Look what you're doing for your wife today. How many people in the nursing home are being chauffeured around Fox Brook Lake? I bet you visit her every day, too."

"Yes, sometimes twice a day," he says to his wife. Then he glares at me. "You remember the other day you told me it was your job to make park visitors have an enjoyable experience?"

"Yes, I'm supposed to."

"Are you supposed to psychoanalyze them?"

Now I know I have overstepped my boundaries, entered his private world and grief... *the Alzheimer's baggageland*. I knew it first hand for almost seven years. He had luxuriated just for an instant about the blue sky, admiring it, just mentioned balloons and his dream, probably a rare moment when he wasn't agonizing about his wife. *Then squelch.*

"No, and I apologize. I guess I said that because after my mother died, well, even before she died, my sleeping mind was trying to work things out."

He looks at the ground, then at his wife. "She had Alzheimer's?"

"Yes, she did."

"Maybe we could talk more some time."

Alzheimer's, the ugly place...

"I really have to focus on the park, though, and my duties."

"Yes, of course."

He shrugs, turns his back to me, buckles his wife into her seat and closes the passenger door. Now the woman looks out at me.

"Going home," she says.

I follow the man to the driver side of his car; he opens the door, climbs in, doesn't start the engine, and won't look at me.

So I lean forward and address the side of his head, "You know sometimes I lack generosity of spirit," I offer. "I told you we're all works in progress. Just consider me unfinished at the moment . . . Sometimes I get stuck . . . Sometimes, well, when I'm patrolling the lake on foot—I can't have

49

passengers in my truck—but you can walk with me and we can talk," I add. And wait. Then persist, "Okay?"

He's tucked up close to the steering wheel, face partially hidden behind the hat, but with a nod he gives his assent.

. . . .

RANGER LOG

Date: July 1

Time: 4 p.m.

... offered assist to disabled woman ... and to her husband ... and invite them back.

. . . .

CHAPTER 6

MARAUDER

Second shift stretches from 4 p.m. until 10 p.m. closing time, sometimes longer if people are still in the park, sometimes shorter if the park is deserted, all depends, lots of discretion there. There is one car in the lot, but no people in sight. It's 10 p.m. and very dark. I suspect skinny dippers, so I do a drive patrol on the bike path that hugs the edge of the lake. Not even a ripple upon the water. Just as I complete my circuit, a young man and woman cross the beach parking lot carrying a blanket. They disappear into their car, and I imagine what took place upon that blanket under the stars, under the canopy of the trees at night.

Except for a few lighted areas, the whole scene is eerily dark, but rife with wildlife. Some county parks provide campsites and the rangers hear tall tales of sounds that entertain the campers at night. Children unzipping the tent flap to peer out into the night, into a set of glowing eyes? "Bear!" they shriek. But I know these parks have no bears, no black bears and certainly no grizzly. *It wouldn't be a bear that would frighten me, anyway.*

The creepiest animal eyes I've ever seen belonged to a creature that the man in the Panama hat brought to the park in his no-kill trap. The generally harmless opossum just wants to be left alone, but, oh my, it is an unattractive animal, like the hairless monkey dog, only even less cuddly.

Assuming an almost shock-like state, it would not come out of the trap. Those eyes didn't even blink. That's where "playing possum" comes from. So the slow moving and nocturnal marsupial with the pointed face, 50 sharp teeth, long hairless tail and a nasty hiss waited motionless until the threat (us) was out of sight. A half an hour later, it had exited the trap and joined the community of Fox Brook Park nocturnal animals.

Most of the animals at Fox Brook are more active after sunset: deer, raccoon, red and gray fox, woodchuck, badger, coyote, skunk, muskrat and rabbits. But the member of the animal kingdom most likely to give a ranger pause in the dark hours is a solitary man.

My first time spotting a lone man in the park, late at night . . .

He drives a pickup truck into the park, after closing. I follow him in my Silverado as he cruises the whole loop from the entrance past the flagpoles and the main beach house, on to the shelter at the north end of the lake, then back and around again. He stops at the flag pole. I stop behind him. Then he exits his truck and walks to the driver side of the Silverado. I remain inside, doors locked.

"Am I doing something wrong?" he inquires. "You've been following me."

I roll down my window. "The park closed at 10 p.m. Why are you driving through the park?"

"Oh, I didn't know about the closing time. I was looking at the county flag you have flying with the American flag. I collect flags. Do you know where I can get one of those?"

Is he kidding? What a convoluted reason to be in the park at night—flag gazing? "You can try calling the Parks Administration Office; see where they buy their flags. Here's a brochure. It has the phone number." I reach across the space that separates the two vehicles and remember my stint as a custard stand car hop, reaching into a car window to deliver change. The heinous customer, probably drunk, bit my arm. That vignette is the reason for quick retraction of my hand.

"Thanks. I appreciate that. I'll be leaving now."

"Have a nice night." *If I hadn't been here, would we notice a missing county flag in the morning? Or would something else be remiss in the park? What's he really doing here?*

. . . .

Satisfied that the park is empty, no vehicles, no visible presence of park patrons, I begin my securing-the-park rituals, the last of which is checking bathrooms in the north shelter which are open until I lock them. Of course, they must be checked before locking; no one would want to spend the night here. I enter the ladies' room and notice a stall in need of toilet paper; another has an overstuffed waste receptacle. Staff will clean bathrooms in the morning, so I leave and turn to lock the door. There is a rattling sound I cannot quite identify. I listen again, but nothing. Night sounds can usually be attributed to animals; mostly I know what they are, so I'm somewhat uncomfortable not identifying this one.

More unnerved than I want to be, I abandon the women's side of the building and move toward the west, the men's washroom. The training: a female ranger must knock on the door and yell, "Ranger" before going in. If a park patron is in there, he'll probably respond or come out. If there is no response, the ranger is free to enter.

I rap three times on the door. "Ranger here."

No response, but suddenly a thud, a loud thump.

I freeze, my skin tingles. I do not open the door. "Is someone in there?"

There is no response and I back away. I approach the door again. *My hands are shaking, damn it.* I lean into the door to listen. There's a sort of whimper and a noise like breathing through a whistle or a straw.

Now I back away again, fear supplanting training. Dark thoughts of a news story, that predator in a bathroom facility in a state park in California; the young boy's throat slashed. And the other story about the dismembered woman . . .

I beat a rapid retreat to the Silverado, get inside, lock the doors, take my radio out of its holster and send a 10-21, a request for the supervisor to call me on my cell.

The phone rings. "Sup, I'm not sure what 10 signal to send you on this. I think someone's in the men's bathroom at the park shelter on the north side—sounded like a fight in there. I didn't go in and the person didn't answer when I knocked and called out. What should I do?"

"Stay in your vehicle. I'll be right there."

I move the Silverado so its headlights are shining on the door to the men's bathroom, then grab my clipboard and scan the 10-signal list for the radio signal I should have sent.

... *10-31 Crime in Progress* ... Maybe ... *10-29 Urgent-use red light and siren* ... Don't know ... *10-33 Emergency* ... Maybe ... *10-96 Mental Subject* ... Pretty likely ... *10-78 Need Assistance* ... Bingo, that's the one I should have used. 10-78.

Anxiety can distort perception and the next few minutes pass like hours; rain increases the gloom. The windshield wipers seem too loud. Still no one is exiting that bathroom.

But here comes the deputy vehicle, cruising right up to the shelter on the bike path. The sup is a retired county sheriff's deputy. He's pursued robbers, rapists, drunks, and murderers. Now he oversees and coaches rangers. *Pretty heavenly assignment. But tonight?*

He's a modern-day Lone Ranger I think. Or a John Wayne western hero. Too tall for his vehicle.

"I'll take care of this," he says. No argument from me. Resolute, he jerks open the men's room door and disappears through the entrance. That thump again, something like a trash can tipping over and my sup yelling "Jesus Christ." I bolt upright.

The biggest raccoon I have ever seen, almost a small bear, lurches out the door way and disappears into the night.

Now it's quiet. I exit the Silverado, stand in the rain, open my umbrella and wait for my sup to reappear.

He leaves the bathroom, locks it, looks at me blankly, and says, "Real rangers don't use umbrellas."

Oops. "What do they do about rain?" *What a stupid question.*

"They have a hat and a rainproof jacket. But, come on, join me in my vehicle."

I'm wearing a hat and a rainproof jacket. What a Mary Poppins ranger flop, using an umbrella, afraid to go into the men's room. I collapse the umbrella and toss it into the back of my truck.

"Remember in training—when you're supposed to call a deputy?"

"Yes. If I am genuinely afraid, that's when I should call."

"And why were you afraid?"

"I saw a man cruising the park earlier. He left, but it was still on my mind, unexplained. I thought there might be two guys in there doing I don't know what. Maybe fighting.

And I felt conflicted because there might be a victim in there and I didn't do anything to help."

"You're unarmed. A ranger isn't a policeman. You're supposed to alert us when policing needs to be done and that's what you did."

"Except it was just a raccoon."

"And now you know what that sounds like, for next time."

"Right," I say as I realize I'm sitting in a squad car for the first time in my life.

"So were those some of the dark thoughts you said you have, the thought that you're failing to protect someone?"

"Sort of. Someone's being murdered inside, and *I don't do enough to stop it.*"

"Whoa, that is a dark one. Someone you know was killed?"

I'm thinking that my mother recently died and that I'm having trouble not believing that she might still be alive if someone had done more. Who is responsible . . . is it me? But I'm not getting into all of that with my sup so I just say "No."

He pushes me more. "Just overly conscientious?"

"How can you be overly conscientious?"

"You can be. It's an actual personality disorder, a syndrome. I don't think that's what your problem is, though."

"I have a problem?"

I wasn't joking, but he's chuckling, a horsey laugh. "Guilt. I know a few things. Guilt and anger."

Man of few words. Gets his point across, though.

"You think you can finish locking up?" is how he concludes.

"Yes, I'll lock up. Then I'm ready to call it a night."

"Okay, Ranger. 10-42."

I exit the squad car and climb into the cab of my truck, drive to the park office where I'll leave the Silverado and drop off my log and give some thought to what the sup said.

Now the once noisy motion of wipers seeming rhythmic and soothing. *That was a lot of noise for a raccoon.* I'd heard them in the dumpsters, noisiest when they're trying to get out. *Why didn't I think it could be raccoons? Maybe because a raccoon can't reach the door handle and pull it. But, if they can climb up the side of a house, and they can, and if they can use those fingerlike paws to unlatch a dumpster lid, they probably can open a door the human way. So it must have been the solitary man who spooked me* . . . I park the car, take out my log. *Avoiding that bathroom door. Was I afraid because of the unknown beyond the door or afraid because it was too familiar? The elevator to the third floor of Mum's nursing home. To allay anxiety over what I might see when the elevator doors parted, I did deep breathing. Inhale . . . and exhale . . . and inhale . . . and exhale . . . and guilt . . . and anger . . . and anger . . . and guilt, let it out, let it out . . .*

I inhale . . . then exhale . . . feel better and make a final log entry.

....

LOG ENTRY

Date: *July 7*

Time: *11 p.m.*

. . . Man driving through park after closing. Said he was interested in acquiring a county flag. Gave him park office brochure for contact phone number. He left park.

. . . Unexplained noises in men's bathroom at north shelter. Called sup. for assist. Was jumbo sized, nimble-fingered raccoon. Park now empty and closed. 10-4.

CHAPTER 7

Summer Girl and Horny Toad

The man in the straw hat and I part ways in advance of a beach drill, my focus now intent on the huge Labor Day weekend crowd, four school bus loads of children from day  camps plus several big family gatherings, the north shelter rented for a wedding, and the green embankment lined with hoards of greased bodies, horny adolescent boys and nearly naked, but for thong bikinis, teenage girls.

The wedding will commence around 1 p.m. and I hope to witness some of it, but that will depend on whether life guards need help at the beach. All patrons are out of the water by 1:10. Then I traverse the shore, stopping to remind toddlers to stay behind the life guard stations as guards practice their rescue drills. Someone from a group of brawny volley ball players has lifted the lid of a beverage cooler revealing opened bottles of beer inside. Drinking alcohol is prohibited, as is glass, on the beach.

"Close your cooler and when you finish this game, take the cooler back to your car," I tell them.

They comply. Now the guards have blown a whistle signifying patrons may return to the water. Kids from the day camps have lined up behind an invisible line parallel to the shore but behind the guard stations. At the sound of the whistle they break for the water like horses out of the gate. No toddlers have been toppled during the stampede and all looks well, so I reposition to the shelter that has been transformed into a chapel.

Now two bouncing, buxom, and noisily cavorting teenage girls ramble up the bike path from the beach. I dart in front of them, put a finger to pursed lips, "Shuussssh. They're getting married," and point to the massive shelter fireplace at the front of what's been transformed into a vision in white. A podium has been placed in front of the hearth and everything else has been decked out in one shade or another of white: rows of white-painted folding chairs, soft white roses attached to each wooden chair that flanks the center aisle where the bride will make her walk to the altar on a white velvet carpet. At the back, the bride herself is being prepped for her entrance, the white organza gown, bouquet of winter white camellias, baby's breath and more white tea roses.

The two teenage girls cover their mouths to stifle giggling and continue their romp into a less populated area of the park, and I free myself for a foot patrol around the perimeter of the lake which brings me back to the wedding at the same time the newlyweds are heading toward an old oak tree to begin the photo sessions. *All the white against the blue, blue sky. Mum used to look out across the lake and then up. "What a beautiful blue sky," she'd marvel.* But I don't want to think of the past and feeling somewhat the interloper anyway, I return my focus to the foot patrol and the overlook that faces south across the lake. There's a shallow sandy point where pedal boats sometime founder, but none of the four boats is stuck today. *Four boats now, used to be five.*

The morning after the mysterious driver of a pick-up truck stopped to admire Fox Brook's county flag, one of the pedal boats went missing. Hauling it away would have required a pickup truck and someone with tools to cut through the chain that tethered the boats one to another. My sup and the foreman reminded me to get names and descriptions in my log, like a description of the vehicle and a license plate number. Either set of details might have assisted police in their unsolved investigation of pedal boat theft.

Now one of the bikini clad girls is alone, seated on a bench overlook. She is crying. Across the lake, I can see the other girl and a teenage boy holding hands, strolling back to the beach.

"Is there something I can do for you?" I ask.

"No." She gulps, then takes a deep breath. "I'm okay."

I dig in my pockets for a handkerchief I know is there somewhere and hand it to the girl, but it dangles in mid air. I set the handkerchief on her lap. The girl picks it up, dabs her eyes and blubbers a meek, "Thank you."

I take that as an invitation, so I sit next to her and ask, "Did you and your girlfriend have an argument?"

The girl giggles, then laughs out loud, a laugh that is half sobbing, but there is some relief expressed in the outburst and at least that's good to hear.

"What happened today?"

"Oh, I guess nothing."

"May I guess? You can tell me if I'm right."

"Okay," she grins with quivering lips.

"You and your girlfriend came here today trolling for boys. That horny boy across the way followed you two like a bee to the honey pot. Then he hooked up with the one he thought more baggable."

"Trolling? Baggable?"

"I guess trolling is a fishing term. I meant maybe you were here to look for boys or have them look for you. And maybe that boy is here looking for girls, particularly the one most likely to let him have his way. The one he can bag. You know, fornication. Sex."

At first she giggles, then the sobbing again.

"Why are you crying? Boys are just like that. Their hormones are driving them. It's no reflection on you."

Then the truth came pouring out. The figure across the lake, the gangly conqueror, was her "boyfriend."

"He *fucked* me," she bawled. "I thought he loved me! And today he just ignores me."

What a coarse word coming out of such a pretty mouth, not that I never heard it at my high school, but here, at the park?

Ordinarily, I'd correct the language at family-oriented Fox Brook, but discretion intervenes. "Oh, I see. Well, that's painful, a hard lesson. Sometimes people get sex and love confused though they go nicely together."

"I don't know what to do. I think I love him, though."

Wow, did this kid's mother not have "the talk" with her. What a teeny bopper . . . in a woman's body.

But feeling inadequate to handle this task, at the same time wanting to get it right, I say, "Trust your feelings. Right now you are feeling pretty hurt. That is yourself talking to you, telling you what's bad and what's good for you. It's not good for you to be having sex right now. I think you were hoping to wind up like that woman you passed down the path."

"Who?"

"The woman getting married today."

Defensive, she insists, "I bet she was having sex before she got married."

"But maybe she was ready because she was in a committed relationship. She wasn't a teenager."

The girl is still sniffling, defensive and avoiding eye contact. I'm wondering if my counsel is doing more harm than good. "Maybe you could talk to your parents about this?"

"Are you kidding me?" she blurts. "They'd go ballistic."

"Is there someone else, an adult you trust?"

"No. Well, I'm talking to you. A park ranger."

Finally a grin on the mascara-smeared face. She turns to me, "Do you, or did you, have teenagers?"

"Did. Boys, though."

"Were they horny toads?"

"Beggars for sex."

More composed now, she asks, "So what are girls supposed to do?"

"How old are you?"

"I'm almost 17."

"So you're a junior or senior?"

"I'll be a senior."

"Then college?"

"My parents think so."

"But you don't know?"

"I don't know . . . My parents are like the Taliban. They won't let me do anything I want to do."

"If your parents were like the Taliban, you wouldn't be wearing that bikini and you would either be married off by now or stoned or flogged. Those are ways some cultures deal with their youth and sex. They marry off the girls right away, and you wouldn't be picking your husband."

"I couldn't stand that."

"You picked that guy across the lake there. How's that working for you?"

Now she's crying again. I'm pushing too hard.

"It happened just once. I wasn't planning on doing it."

Should I be giving this girl parental guidance? Seems beyond rangering. But she's a little human being and she's suffering, so I go on.

"A guidance counselor at the high school you go to—I used to work there—told me that most girls who had sex with their boyfriends the first time weren't planning on having sex. Usually drinking was involved and then someone's family room, the kids left alone. In other words, at home."

"Yup, that's pretty much how it happened, after his graduation party."

"I think you know you made a mistake. Tell your parents. They'll be glad you learned from the experience. They might be upset at first, but I'm sure they love you in a way that's more genuine than the 'love' you got from your boyfriend."

"Absolutely not."

" . . . to 920," the radio blurts, call coming from the park foreman. The lifeguards need help at the beach.

"Geez, I have to get back to the beach. Why don't you come with me?"

"No, I'll just sit here a while. I'm okay. Thanks for talking to me."

"But maybe walking a bit would be good."

"No," she says into the crumpled handkerchief which she suddenly recognizes as not her own and pushes toward me.

"You keep the handkerchief and take care of yourself. Don't give your heart away." *What an inadequate thing to say.* I don't like leaving the girl; I turn and call back, "Come to the park again tomorrow. We can talk some more."

The girl waves with the handkerchief and replies, barely audibly, "Awesome!" but she is not smiling.

. . . .

RANGER LOG

Date: *Oct. 1*

Time: *2:30 p.m.*

Checked on wedding at north shelter, comforted upset teenage girl (boyfriend problems) at 1:30 p.m. Helped distraught mother locate missing daughter. Emergency ended 2 p.m.

. . . .

Ranger supervisors are as busy as rangers on weekends, most frequently at the parks with overnight camping, but on this occasion, a month after Labor Day, the sup makes an evening stop at Fox Brook, not to check on rangers or drinking or parking infractions; it's to convey, in person, an administrative concern. A patron has complained about me.

"Can you tell me the name of the person who complained?" I ask the sup.

"No. But this isn't the first time there was an incident in the park and you didn't get the patron's name. If you had, you could figure out who complained."

"But it wasn't really an incident. No injuries, no violations. Just a conversation. I was trying to comfort the girl."

"I'm supposed to tell you that the complaint is on record and, yes, I know you don't care, but it's too bad because you've been rather exemplary outside your occasional *I don't care* which is just a cover for you do care but you're pissed off about something."

I don't like the scold. "What does the complaint say?"

"That you used inappropriate language, that you gave the girl advice about birth control."

"Wow. She must have talked to her parents after all. She said they'd go ballistic and they did. I'd like to invite that girl's parents to the beach, take a look at what the girls, including their daughter, are wearing there, how the boys are behaving, what kind of messages are going back and forth. She should take a peek at what I see at night when it's dark and the beach is closed. I consider what I told the girl a real favor to her. The parents have their heads stuck in the sand."

"It isn't your job, though and, besides, the girl didn't exactly talk to them. They found out she's pregnant and they confronted her."

I think *what has that got to do with me* but ask, "And they think I helped that happen?"

"What's behind this is they think it happened here at the park, that if the ranger had been doing her job, well, you know the script. They want to know who the guy is, too. Do you know?"

"Not, as per usual unfortunately, not his name, but she said he was her boyfriend. . . . I might add, she used the 'F' word, not me. I saw the horny toad she had sex with from across the lake. He was tall and lanky, had kind of reddish hair. She didn't mention his name. I think he had just graduated."

"There might be some follow-up on that."

"But I didn't do anything illegal or unethical. Plus, she didn't have sex with him here. She told me that! And I thought my discretion was appropriate, too."

"You know what they say. Perception is everything. And we are employed by the taxpaying public. Anyway, that's where things stand at the moment. Don't give the parents anything more to complain about."

"I probably won't even see that girl again," I say but don't mean.

"Just be a ranger."

"Okay," I acquiesce, tentatively, "10-4." My hesitation over a more enthusiastic 10-4 means I'm not really checking out. The summer girl has become part of a growing but unanticipated collection, a menagerie of compelling park folks I find myself caring about. Season one has ended, but the surprises haven't even begun.

SEASON TWO

2007

CHAPTER 8

BICYCLE MENACE

In Shakespeare's *Julius Caesar*, Mark Anthony stirs up the crowd with a reading. The will of Julius Caesar has promised every individual citizen of Rome Caesar's "park property" . . .

> He hath left you all his walks,
> His private arbors and new-planted orchards,
> On this side Tiber; he hath left them you
> And to your heirs forever-common pleasures,
> To walk abroad and recreate yourselves.

For Romans who had no such property of their own, such a bequeathal could not have come from a man who deserved to be stabbed more than 20 times by his colleagues. This benefactor's death would be avenged. The suddenly loyal Romans tore limbs off more than a few innocents in the civil war that followed.

Fox Brook history hasn't that much drama, but it bears mentioning that on big picnicking holidays like the 4th of July, ordinary residents utilize the park. People with 1.3 acre back yards and swimming pools gather at home. Property owners with lake cottages "up north" are up north! People without such resources have an attractive alternative, though. Apartment dwellers with large, extended families but small living quarters, teenagers with plenty of energy but no volleyball court, residents with labs and retrievers, but no swimming holes, the park is a low cost remedy.

For Billie the ranger, more people equal more problems, and the exercise of discretion seems more complex this 4th of July. Solutions generally involve carefully choosing battles. For example, an indignant father accompanied by his very young daughters complains, "There's a kid fully exposing his male parts." I look over the crowded beach to the picnicking grounds beyond and see two young women, maybe the boy's mother and sister or aunt or friend, and a little boy whose diaper has been removed. The young boy's caregivers giggle over the tyke's urinating while gallivanting in on the lawn. The toddler is indeed running in circles, penis definitely exposed, but freedom—not obscenity—seems to be the source of his glee. No ill intent that I observe. The man complains the boy is "of age," whatever that means, and his girls should not have to be exposed to such a scene. His little girls and their mother are lying on a blanket now, the girls gawking at the mini spectacle.

By the time I arrive at this scene of suburban pornography, the boy has been diapered and the young girls have lost interest. There's no point in harassing the women. They haven't broken any laws; their parenting styles have clashed with their neighbors'. That the man is white and his daughters are blond, that the women are Hispanic and the little boy well endowed, that the park is in an affluent white neighborhood of a largely politically conservative county, none of those variables should matter, but I'm a ranger who lives on planet Earth and decide discretion in this case means leave it alone. I return to what might be more pressing problems on the beach.

Two agitated teenage girls approach. Kids are genuinely upset when they want help from an adult wearing a uniform. "Someone is hiding in the bushes and blowing a bullhorn whenever someone walks by," one announces.

The other one says, "And when someone cycles past he does it, too."

I head south of the beach to the bike path location of the mystery menace, and I'm wondering if a good ranger breaks into a run on an occasion like this because I don't arrive soon enough. The perpetrator and an accomplice have scurried up the railroad embankment and over the rails beyond the southern boundary of the park into relative obscurity and safety: a residential neighborhood. At least I observed some identifying details: the boy is tall, hair dyed red, white and blue for the holiday, and he's wearing red shorts and a white T-shirt.

After returning to the beach, I hear the elephantine bullhorn and know the menace returned after my brief pursuit and later, while patrolling the west end of the lake, a lifeguard radios, "A biker's on the beach with a bullhorn and he's mimicking life guard commands."

Back to the east end I go, to the beach house, out of sight of the menace. I radio the park foreman. "The kid's tall, red-headed, has on red shorts, white T-shirt and a bullhorn, probably taken from a life guard station."

"10-4." Within seconds an off road vehicle from the direction of the park office is careening past a bike trail to an overlook where the menace and his sidekick have parked their bikes and somehow ditched the bullhorn. The park foreman thrusts himself in front of the primary suspect who is standing on the edge of the quarry. You could say the kid was trapped. I observe he makes no attempt to flee; he's smiling. Gloating.

Then the foreman radios me. There will be "a talk."

. . . .

The world is better off with one less errant cyclist on the boardwalk, I recall. But the errant rider is very much still here and certainly hasn't improved his behavior. He's looking at me now in uniform—no recognition—maybe because he had never focused on my face in the first place, but I remember him. The sullen boy with the Micargi, the Micargi I tossed into the bog. Now, confronted by authority, the menace denies having hassled anyone, even though the head life guard has just confirmed, "Yup, that's the kid."

"I could call a sheriff deputy to ticket you for disturbing the peace," the foreman threatens which strikes fear into the heart of the menace's friend who says, "I'll go home now." But the spiky-haired tall one looks more like he's just been challenged, not threatened. He shrugs, still cocky, grinning. Both boys bike away, the menace triumphant, I think, as he has experienced no consequences other than a warning, and he's upset a host of park employees and patrons.

"I've seen the cocky one before. He usually comes alone and amuses himself by terrorizing the park. That's how I knew where to find him when you radioed," the foreman offers, and I wonder why the kid is tolerated.

I had never seen a park patron issued a ticket for anything other than parking violations. I'd like to issue citations myself for dog infractions. And the young rider of a red bike isn't rattled by the specter of a sheriff's deputy because, so far, the threats have been empty. Most intriguing to the me, if somewhat unsettling, is his attitude might be due, at least in small part, to the incident known as the bog bike, which, of course, makes me an accomplice in the impoverishment of his personality.

. . . .

The menace does come back the next day, bullhorn and all, but the foreman doesn't want to call a deputy. Maybe he has reason to avoid extra-departmental scrutiny. Maybe, like me, he wants to manage problems himself, call in the authorities when he's exhausted other avenues.

I ask, "Why don't you call a deputy?"

"What has he done? He's not drunk. He hasn't assaulted anyone."

"Disturbing the peace?"

"Let's say someone calls the media, like someone from the American Civil Liberties Union, or just the local press—can't you see it? Park foreman picks on young boy. Takes away his right to enjoy a public park when all the boy did was make a little exuberant noise. The boy is unarmed and hurting no one, not drinking, and a sheriff deputy is called to the scene? I'd be portrayed as the bully turning away perfectly good kids of the tax-paying public."

But he has the boy's name. He calls his parents instead.

The mother says she'll come over with her husband, the boy's father; he's coming home for lunch. The son won't expect to see him. She emphasizes that her son shouldn't be told his father is coming. *Why not?*

The boy, if he is worried, certainly isn't showing any fear. He lies to the foreman about using a bullhorn and about his home phone number, but the foreman got it anyway, on file from the missing bike incident report.

When father and mother arrive, the son sees them, gets on his bike and begins to peddle away, not with any speed, accelerating just enough to be physically out of reach. He glances behind, sees his father waving him back. His view: park foreman, ranger and both parents. For the first time, the menace, perhaps realizing the futility of his flight, is hesitant. He returns.

At this point, the foreman takes over. He tells the unhappy little family he could ban the boy from Foxbrook; the boy says "I don't care" –the old *doesn't care*, camouflage for *cares very much*, cover for *feels a lot of pain*-and he says it to his father. He may have said, "I don't care," but to his father's ears it was, "I don't care about YOU, I don't respect YOU."

The father's face turns red, jaw tightens, fists clench; he assumes a stance the ranger remembers from training. The stance is an alert: *aggression*. He even starts to raise a fist.

"You don't care?" he spits, the rage palpable.

Now the foreman wants to de-escalate. He doesn't want a domestic assault to add to problems he's already got in the park today. He offers a conciliatory third chance at the park. Parents are in agreement that the offer is more than fair. The boy agrees, too. He's had another incident with no real consequences. What's not to agree with?

The boy pedals out of the park as his parents make their way back to their Humvee.

"A Humvee? Who drives a Humvee anymore?" I ask the foreman.

"A military type. Probably an Afghanistan or Iraq veteran. The dad's probably a vet, of course."

"Of course? What has military to do with this?"

"It may have everything to do with what happened today. Did you see that father?" The foreman is pushing his hair back from his perspiring forehead and rearranging his cap. He's relieved. He knows the outcome could have been worse. "He was on the brink of a physical assault on his kid."

"Yeah, and right in front of us. Imagine what he might have done at home, without witnesses or an audience."

"Imagine what he's already done at home," the foreman reflects out loud.

. . . .

The afternoon's anxieties abate with the exit from the park of the menace and his parents, and I've had time to both decompress and contemplate the boy and his probably like-minded father.

My last year of teaching I'd had a student with ALS, the *Tuesdays with Morrie* disease, very rare in a person so young. If I passed out a quiz or assignment, the girl in the first seat of Jimmy's row said, "One more, please. Jimmy's comin'." When I returned papers, someone in the back of the room, near the door would point to Jimmy's empty desk and expect me to place his papers there, "He's comin'."

He was a physically weak kid, walked unsteadily and was usually late for class. I told my class, "Tardiness is a form of rudeness and rudeness is disrespect." But I hadn't been targeting this boy and told him in private that he did not need to apologize for tardiness. But he wasn't looking to be exempted from rules, no sense of entitlement.

Eventually Jimmy would appear in the doorway, using the frame and the wall to support himself as he navigated to his desk. Then the quiet, "Sorry I'm late." His condition deteriorated, and finally he just could not make those walks between classrooms anymore. He succumbed to a wheelchair. To him that was capitulation, defeat.

I had never seen kids in my class treat him disrespectfully. I never saw bullying or ridicule, snickers or condescension. They protected him.

What would the Fox Brook bully in my classroom have been like?

. . . .

Later, at my desk in the park office, I'm wondering how much of all of this day's events I need to record in my log. Most of it will probably end up in my journal, my record of progress *filling the void*. I pick up the journal and page back to entries made during a teacher in-service on bullying.

"What's that? All that your log?" the foreman at the desk behind me mutters.

"My journal, notes. I've been reading them. I think that dad from today might be a bully, you know, clinically. People used to think all bullying comes from low self-esteem. But no. Now the bully brains say what they lack,

I'm reading from my notes, 'is compassion, empathy and impulse control. Bullying is their . . .' I have a hard time reading my own writing, 'anger management technique. They enjoy cruelty.'"

"So the kid's been bullied at home."

" 'Or he may have observed his parents,'" I continue to read, " 'express prejudices and view other people as competitors standing in their way.' So the kid learns that aggression is rewarded and respected, humiliating others is tolerated. 'Compassion and empathy are weaknesses.'"

"My take on the psycho babble: The guy probably has post traumatic stress syndrome from a war experience," the foreman concludes.

"But look," I plow through scribbled notes, "some characteristics of the bully: 'no empathy, control freak, denial, charm, glib, compulsive lying, devious, manipulative.'"

Tiring of the tutorial, the foreman concedes, "Okay, he's a bully."

But what sounds like pedantic fervor to the foreman seems like a mystery solved to me, " ' . . . superior sense of invulnerability, untouchability, evasive, undermines anyone he perceives to be an adversary or a threat.' And just one more thing, 'he may pursue a vindictive vendetta against anyone who attempts to hold him accountable.'"

"Well, that would be you and me. So what's the cure for the kid?"

"I don't know. That kid's going to come back for more, you know."

The foreman sighs. "That dad was really mad. What an ugly face anger has."

. . . .

In the ranger office at park closing time, the foreman long gone, I set aside my closed log, then open my journal again to the bullying in-service notes. Leaning back and looking up, I close my eyes and recall being bumped off the boardwalk but not by the character who turned out to be the park menace. *Park menace and boardwalk racer.* I smile to myself, but amusement at the twofold bully identity wanes. There is something else that doesn't feel right. I had engaged in some cruelty myself, an act of evening the score. It wasn't compulsive, but it was devious. Certainly wasn't compassionate. And it may have aggravated the already distorted perceptions the park menace had of the people in his universe.

I write in my journal, "The ugly face that anger has? It's my face. I'm going to apologize."

CHAPTER 9

PARK RESCUE

One annual essential for rangers is first aid certification. Most often the aid dispensed is a Band-Aid for a cut or a bruise, something minor; that's what the first aid kit is for. The bigger issue is cardio pulmonary resuscitation. All hope never to have to use the defibrillator, but all train for the eventuality, a park patron whose heart has stopped beating. Annie the rubber woman—really a mannequin whose rising and falling chest simulates a real human chest cavity—has a rounded orifice of an artificial mouth that elicits lurid remarks and giggles from trainees who must provide her oxygen; she is the park patron who has stopped breathing.

By the end of the day, rangers must demonstrate mastery of resuscitation including the correct timing of air exchange for a 6-year-old, then maybe a 60-year-old, even an infant. And the refresher course is necessary. Details not needed on a day-to-day basis are easily forgotten: first check for breathing and for pulse; don't start breathing for the victim before you've checked for an obstruction in the throat, etc. Chest compression is a method for moving blood through a victim who might otherwise suffer brain oxygen deprivation and death before paramedics arrive with a defibrillator. These compressions aren't expected to restart the heart like you see in so many movies, but they might save a life. A defibrillator certainly can. So rangers carry a portable defibrillator in their park vehicles. Know: left from right, basically, where to attach the paddles, when to clear. And get the defibrillator to the victim as soon as possible.

. . . .

I'm always grateful to encounter no injuries and up until today, I've treated only a few scratches requiring Band Aids. Today the park is packed with people and heat is oppressive. I do a foot patrol to check for swimmers and dogs in unauthorized areas and wonder if the man in the Panama hat is going to bring his wife to the park on a day as hot and humid as this. I'd like to see him, the cheerful countenance, his glass half full, not half empty. How else could he keep smiling through his wife's Alzheimer's and her care at the nursing home? So it is with delight that I happen upon the woman on the path in her transport chair. *Who is pushing the chair? Where is her husband? He left her alone here?*

She is near the path to the north shelter, facing the men's room. I knock on the door.

"Is anyone in there?" No answer. I open the door. No man in a Panama hat.

I kneel in front of the woman. "What happened to your husband?" She is leaning precariously forward, with her feet out of the stirrups, trying to pull herself and the chair forward in a sort of tippy-toe gripping of the pavement. But she cannot articulate the source of her anxiety. The man with the straw hat must be in some kind of trouble, so I return the woman's feet to the stirrups, grasp the handles in back of the chair, spin the chair around and propel the woman and her chair back in the other direction, toward the north parking lot.

Near the overlook on the north side of the lake, a heap on the side of the path may have impressed a passerby as a bag of uncollected garbage. But there is the identifying straw hat. The heap is a man.

I leave the woman and the transport chair and crouch down near the man's face. He is breathing but unresponsive, unconscious, his face grimaced, one side pulled down in a frown. *Maybe a stroke.* With pulse and heartbeat presenting, no need for the defibrillator. And good thing because I am on a foot patrol, the defibrillator in my vehicle a half mile away, the park foreman and the lifeguard gone for the day. *I'm on my own.*

I grab my cell, dial 911, then unholster my radio. I could do a 10-52, *ambulance needed*, but the 911 operator says an ambulance is already on its way. I radio the sup, 10-21, *request for a phone call*. I hear, already, a siren from a rescue vehicle; it's already in the park.

My cell rings; I tell the sup an ambulance is on the way for a park patron who is barely conscious.

"Maybe he's had a stroke, I don't know. There are just a few things I don't get, though. I know the man and his routine. His car is here. It's 5:30. I don't think I've ever seen him here with his wife this late before."

"So what are you saying?"

"I'm saying maybe his collapse isn't from natural causes. I'm not sure what to report to the police."

"Can his wife tell you anything?"

The wife's face is tight, her posture tense. She is fixated on her husband who is still on the ground. She keeps gripping the pavement with her toes, her hands clasped tightly to the sides of her chair, moving toward him.

"She's got Alzheimer's. Right now she's pretty agitated, confused. I don't know if she knows that is her husband there. I think she does. She's trying to reach him."

"Billie, let the professionals handle it, but record all the details in a report. You're not the police. You're a witness right now. I'll be over there in a few minutes."

"10-4."

I kneel beside the man, hold one hand. He pulls it away and groans. I realize I may have hurt him. Maybe his hand was injured in the fall. His face, on the right side is swollen, too. The fall?

I shift my focus to the woman, take one of her hands from its grip on the chair and hold it, lean in close to her face.

"What happened to him? Can you tell me?"

I know an Alzheimer's victim's short term memory is the first great loss. If she knew what happened to him five minutes ago, it might all be lost by now. Maybe. But sometimes not. *So much not known about Alzheimer's.*

"If you can remember what you saw, I wish you would tell me."

The woman's pupils are dilated. *What would cause that? Emotional trauma? What meds is she on?*

I can see the ambulance now, it is only seconds away. The man with the straw hat has rolled over unto his side. The back pockets of his jeans are visible. They are empty.

Paramedics take over, and I'm relieved.

But they need to know his name. I have always called him the man with the straw hat or the Panama hat. *I never got his full name. What is wrong with me?* They can't find ID on him. *So his wallet is gone. He must have driven his wife here; he would ordinarily have a wallet with driver's license. No wallet, no ID.*

"His wife should have an ID bracelet from her nursing home," I think out loud. A paramedic rolls up her left sleeve. There is the plastic ID bracelet. A red dot indicates she is a "do not resuscitate" resident of her nursing home.

The authorities will contact Riversite, get the man's full name, get her back to the home and get him to the hospital.

And I will write an incident report.

. . . .

Later, in the Silverado, I peruse my journal and the bullying notes, make an additional journal entry:

"The sup and the foreman and the police and I talked about foul play. Of course, I was to continue to be just a ranger and leave the investigation to the professionals, yadda, yadda. Don't get all involved.

But I cannot forget the man in the Panama hat or ignore the fact of an accident or worse, the missing wallet, and the ambulance having already been called before I called in. But also, the man's daily advocacy for his wife has now come to an end. And I know all too well what that might mean for her welfare and how important her welfare is to him. I am already involved."

. . . .

By 6:30 p.m., the man has been transported to the hospital, his wife has been transported to Riversite, and everyone has their reports. Back on the beach, which is visible from the overlook where the unconscious man was found, I can see Merlin searching the sand with his metal detector.

I know I'll be talking to him next.

CHAPTER 10

CONVERSATION WITH MERLIN

His name is Merwyn, but I call the white-bearded, soft-spoken senior Merlin the Metal Man. His stooped posture places his face close to the beach he's  scouring with his wand, his magical metal detector, simple pleasures, simple man. Always he can count on harvesting a few quarters but also big hauls like class rings—his favorite. From a ring he can gather enough information to contact the school, ID the ring's owner, get a mailing address and then reunite the ring and its owner. His highest highs are the letters of thanks he gets from the ring recoverers. His lowest low was the one ring owner who never acknowledged his random act of kindness.

After the barely conscious man in the Panama hat is sent off to the hospital and his wife to Riversite, the reports written and the scene quiet, I return to the Silverado and drive to the beach, now deserted except for the wizened and ring-bearing Merlin.

"What was all the commotion about, Billie?"

"That's what I was going to ask you. Before the ambulance came, did you see anyone near the picnic shelter or on the bike path there? Anything at all?"

He leans on his detector; it functions as his cane, too. "No, I was kind of focused on my hunt here. A bike rider went by, in the direction of the picnic shelter, but that's all I can think of."

"I don't suppose you noted the time."

"Just, now that you ask, it was before the ambulance came, but not long before."

"And then did you see him come around the lake on the other side?"

"No, but I wasn't looking, either. I'm mainly looking down. Here the buzz? I got something!" He proffers it to me, "Here, you can have this one."

"It's a pop top from a can. Patrons shouldn't be leaving those on the beach. Hey, you're kind of useful, Merlin. I'm recommending you get a fee from the county for vacuuming the beach."

Merlin thinks I'm serious. "Naw, I don't need the money. I'm on social security now. I don't need no more money. I just like getting them thank you letters."

"Well, maybe you could get some thank you's from the county now, too."

"Oh, that I wouldn't mind." He begins to come out of his stoop, but not without considerable effort.

"Can you recall anything else about that biker?"

"He was biking fast."

"Racing bike?"

"Yup, if them thin bikes are racing bikes, and he was racing." He uses his free arm to cut through the air, "Whoosh."

"Describe the bike?"

"Red. I don't know bike brands, though."

"What about the cyclist?"

"Just a young guy; I don't know. Why? What happened over there?"

"A man was with his wife. She's in a wheelchair. The man collapsed. I found him barely conscious on the bike path. The ambulance took him to the hospital and someone took his wife back to her nursing home. The guy may have had a stroke; I don't know."

"Yah, maybe the biker went by before he fell down."

"Maybe the biker knocked him down."

"Ho, I didn't even think of that."

"It does happen."

"I have a hard time believing someone would do that, just leave and all."

I think how lucky Merlin is to believe no one would do a hit and run. "That's cause you're such a nice guy, Merlin. Anyway, if you saw that cyclist on his bike again, do you think you'd know him?"

"Maybe, if he went by on that red bike, real fast again."

"If he does, if you see him, would you mind letting me know? I'd like to ask him a few questions. Here's my card. It has my cell phone number on it. You can use that to call me even if I'm not in the park."

He takes the card. "They have rangers doing investigations now?"

"No. I'm just . . . you know how you like to be helpful, don't have to be paid to feel good about it? That's me, too."

"Yup. I know what you mean. Okay, I'll watch for the cyclist. Heh, though, maybe the cyclist is the one who called 911."

"That's a thought." And it's one that hadn't occurred to me, although the 911 operator had said an ambulance was already on the way.

"Just call me Sherlock. Ha!"

"Why wouldn't the cyclist stick around after he called 911?" I thought my question would challenge Merlin's naiveté.

But Merlin can't be checked. "Cause he might get blamed? Cause he don't trust nobody? Sounds like he's already read *your* mind, like he knows you're gunnin' for him?"

That made me recall the nursing assistant's epiphany at my mother's nursing home: "Just cause they quiet don't mean they stupid."

Merlin isn't as simple as he sounds.

CHAPTER 11

LEAVING IT TO THE PROFESSIONALS: RIVERSITE

The Man in the Panama hat recovered. Although tests were inconclusive, doctors attributed Dave Cato's collapse to heat stroke. That was the word in the park, anyway. It had been late in the afternoon that day, 95 degrees with matching high humidity and Dave Cato, pushing the wheelchair,  taxed his 79-year-old body. It momentarily quit on him.

He can't recall what happened to his wallet. "I'm forgetting stuff more lately, but not like my wife does. I didn't eat my dinner. I was later than usual because Alice didn't want to go anywhere until she'd had her dinner; she was pretty firm, actually kind of combative, on that point." He's wearing out.

And since that close call, he worries more about Alice, about what could happen to her if he died . . . her vulnerability, her dependence on strangers, can't remember her caregivers, doesn't even know who to ask for help. And so sweet, he thinks, she apologizes for forgetting their names.

"I have twenty minutes for lunch; join me at the park office, Dave."

He's early today and without his wife who is probably at lunch at Riversite. Geographic change is becoming more difficult for her. Even if he can get Alice in and out of his car, he has to deal with her confusion at a restaurant. She shrieks at the menu, "The prices! I don't have that kind of money!"

Seventy-six-year-old Alice thinks she's 36 and must expect a 40-year-old menu. No $.25 cups of coffee anymore. For Dave, lunch out with Alice is an exercise in patient reassurance.

"Don't worry about the prices. Let me worry about that." I hope he doesn't have to worry about money, too.

I've retrieved my bag lunch from the office refrigerator. Dave is seated at a picnic bench, expectant. I pop the lids on two cokes.

"Have one?"

"No, I had breakfast. Need to talk." His arms are crossed in front of his chest. He's bracing for something.

"I can see that. What's on your mind?"

"I don't like the staff where Alice is. The social worker keeps trying to persuade me to move her up to the third floor. She says that's where the dementia people are concentrated and that care is better that way and it's more quiet, but the residents say it's the death ward. It's where they put the truly mortal ones. There was even a fire set up there once. The staff doesn't say much about that, but residents tell me someone deliberately set it."

"How do they know someone deliberately set it?" I bluster.

"It was in the nurse's station. You can't even get a wheelchair in that space. Plus one of the residents said a woman who wasn't staff had been there that night. He thinks she did it. But when the police asked him who she was, he said he didn't know, had never seen her before. They asked him to describe her. He said, 'Describe who?' The police concluded he was senile. But one of his caregivers told me that resident was a sheepshead player. I never heard of a senile person who could play sheepshead."

Bless that resident's little heart. "So what do you want to talk to me about, Dave?"

"Remember when you asked me if my wife had been falling and I said yes and you knew it had been on a weekend and that the nursing home had told me she had a fall?"

"Yes."

"How did you know it happened on a weekend?"

I defer answering the question and agitate Dave by adjusting the pita wrap around my tuna salad. He's tapping his feet now.

"Don't you want that Coke?" I point to the opened can. He's waiting.

"Nope," his terse response. "I want you to answer the question."

I take a deep breath because in a war of attrition with Dave, I will lose. Dave's arms still crossed in front of his chest, he's leaning forward toward me, so I plunge in.

"On weekends the regular professional staff, let's call it the A team, is usually not there. 'Pool' nurses are standing in. Supervision of staff is loose and free, at least from what I could see. And that means monitoring of residents is loose, too. My mother was discharged from the hospital back to the nursing home on a weekend. I feared her movements wouldn't be safely monitored and they weren't. She had four falls—and those are the ones that were reported . . . eventually the physical therapy people got her an automated talking device that reminded her to sit down when she would start to get up from her chair. But first she had to have a bunch of falls. I still feel bad about that."

"Like you didn't do enough?"

"Even worse than that. I never knew what I'd walk into when the elevator door opened. One time she was in her chair and the alarm was repeating, 'Sit down, Joan. Sit down, Joan . . .' and she *was* sitting down and answering, 'I *am* sitting . . .' completely confused and distressed. And what was most disturbing is she thought it was me, my voice tormenting her."

"Why didn't someone turn off the alarm?"

"Don't even get me started. Why don't they do a lot of things. I'm sure you have seen things that give you pause. Do you feel like you're doing enough for Alice?"

"No, I don't."

Dave is looking older, head tilted to one side, brow heavy. Neither of us speaks for a long moment.

"What else?"

So I continue, "I mean you read in the paper all the time about new developments in dementia care, recommendations, task forces. I cut out a lot of articles. Creating cultures of safety, of caring. I think if we were talking about children, more would be done. But old people, you, well not you, but people don't think the elderly are important. I shouldn't be saying this to you. You're living it."

"Did you think of moving her to a different home?" he asks.

"Yes. Actually Riversite had no citations from regulators the year my mother was first admitted. But the next year it had a change in management and then a change in ownership. How can you know in advance when that's going to happen? One home that a friend recommended, someone whose husband had been there, closed because it ran out of money. The issue is always money. Maybe you find what you think is a great nursing home and there are no Medicaid beds. So then you get on a waiting list."

"Alice's on Medicaid now. I ran out of money." That doesn't surprise me, but Dave Cato seems embarrassed.

"I read that about 75 percent of long term care residents are on Medicaid," I tell him. "I mean even if you weren't indigent going in, you might be going out, at 7-10 thousand dollars a month, over the number of years that an Alzheimer's patient can live? You can be relatively self sufficient and then lose it all. But, at least in Wisconsin, you as the spouse can keep your home."

"I'm not so worried about that. I would just like to have her in a better place."

"You mean like 'Founders Village'? Have you ever been to that one, Dave?"

"They don't have Medicaid beds available."

"Okay, you have been shopping. We looked into Founders Village before we placed my mother at Riversite. I saw an old man in a hallway; he looked confused, was standing with a walker. A nurse or nurse aide had his arm. She said something to him that ended with, 'Don't you remember?' To which he replied, 'If I could remember, I wouldn't be here.' And this at a nursing home that promises a staff well trained in dementia care."

"I've lost count the number of times I've heard a caregiver say, 'Don't you remember?' to Alice."

"Anyway, it's not a safe place for Alice, a place where so little monitoring takes place that a fire gets started and no one knows how. If I sold my home—and it is lake property—I could afford to put her in a private facility, like CompassionCare Home."

"That's all wealthy people," I gasp. "They don't accept Medicare or Medicaid. The costs are astronomical. Where would you live if you sold your home?"

"I'd think of something. I don't need much."

"Your sons?"

"They wouldn't want to lose the real estate, see it go. But it's Alice's house, too."

"There goes their inheritance?"

"Yes, and they think her care is adequate where she is, and that I'm just having trouble letting go."

"Riversite is a one-star rated facility now," I add. "That means it got an 'F' from state inspectors. And still operating."

Dave's leaning into the table now, his arms uncrossed, open. "I have a will. Maybe I need to do more with that too. There's nothing in there about my wife's nursing home care. What do they call the person who's supposed to make sure the terms of the will are met?"

"The executor."

"I think I'd better make a few changes. The executor has to change—need someone who will advocate for Alice." Dave's relaxed now, fingering his CocaCola can, thinking.

"Have you met Tuma, the aide from Ethiopia?" I ask.

"Yes, he's the best one. I wish he were there 24-7."

"I think if you took all the best practices of nurses, put them in a blender, added a bit of chocolate and some genuine Christian compassion, you'd get Tuma. He told me his aging parents and their friends and relatives in Ethiopia had no transportation to their new church 15 miles from their village. So what did Tuma do? He used all his savings, $10,000 and $20,000 more that his church here kicked in, and bought a used bus he found on the internet, somehow got it shipped to Ethiopia, and now those old Ethiopian villages are driven to church every Sunday.

"He puts his hand on his heart whenever he talks about his family. Talk about a caregiver by nature. He told me that caregivers know you're coming every day; they know you're going to be asking questions about care. And that you know their names. Your presence does mean better care."

"Yeah, I hope I can keep that up, going every day."

He also said you can get bad care in a good home as well as good care in a bad one. But Dave Cato doesn't need to hear that. Where ever Alice is he'll advocate for good care. So I just caution him, "But, Alice still has Alzheimer's and when you move her, she'll be confused. Hope you've given this a lot of thought."

"My sons say I think about it too much."

"Yes, well, a will and a trust. Have a good talk with an estate planning lawyer. Good investment, the kind that will give you some peace of mind which, just incidentally, might make *you* live longer."

"I'd like to have the peace of mind that comes from knowing I did everything I possibly could."

"I hear you."

" . . . I think you do . . . and you were an advocate. Isn't that some comfort to you now?"

I take another deep breath. "I was gone for 7 days, in Florida with my husband. That's when she got really sick, I mean gravely ill. The nurse who called—she left a message on my answering machine—told me some kind of gastrointestinal flu spread through the home. They called me; they're required by law to do that, to tell me she was vomiting, on Friday. I got back on Sunday. I took one look at her . . . I asked them to call an ambulance and send her to a hospital emergency room. The hospital admitted her . . . critical condition, dehydrated and her kidneys were failing. It was too late to save her.

Dave is incredulous, "Hadn't someone been checking on her?"

"The home put her on 24 hour report. That means they check her vital signs, blood pressure, temperature, respiration, or they're supposed to, each shift. The 'normal' range, I learned later, is broad . . . and, well, you spend a lot of time there, Dave. You think they do all that? When a lot of residents are sick and the staff gets busy and some of them are working 16 hour shifts, and they're not supervised . . . do you think they actually do all those things?"

"I have a great fear of that."

"Later, I reported the whole incident to the state, to the regulatory branch and they sent out an inspector to investigate. She spent a couple days at the home, looking at records, interviewing staff. I looked at records I requested from the home, too. I saw 'encouraged hydration' recorded with regularity. That is how the nursing home covers its bases, legally. But I never saw anyone actually encouraging my mother or her roommate to drink, just a CNA placing a cup of ice water in the room. My mother didn't know it was her cup, much less filled with water she was supposed to drink. Her roommate was bedridden and couldn't reach her water; she'd ask me to bring it to her. But the aides put water in her room, so they've *encouraged hydration*.

"Anyway, the inspector's report said she 'couldn't prove that any codes had been violated.' Are you surprised?"

He shakes his head. I don't know if he's answering the question or just expressing disbelief.

I'm starting to feel drained but can't stop, "My sister was there once or twice that week. My two nieces spent time with her on other days. Her old friend Ian came up from Florida to visit her, too. Someone saw her every day. Even state inspectors were there that week, doing observations for Medicare ratings. She still fell through the cracks. And it happened while I was gone."

"So all those people involved plus the nursing home and you still blame yourself."

"No, not just me. There's plenty of blame to go around. But that not-having-done-enough sentiment? You've got it, too. That's part of grieving, I'm told. My dreams plagued me, seeing her so deteriorated and no one getting excited about it. I couldn't escape even in sleep. Remember your dream about the dog falling out of a balloon?"

A grim nod.

"The night the ambulance took my mother to the hospital, I dreamed I saw a massacre, someone hacking off someone's limbs, people walking right by, not seeing it. I'm horrified and no one shares my horror because no one sees it. I try to get someone's attention, but no one seems particularly excited, just me. Then Mum wanders aimlessly through nursing home, me following her, no one paying attention. She walks to the end of a hall which is a precipice, falls off into a body of water. She doesn't know that she won't be able to breathe down there, and I don't know how to rescue her, and I'm telling her not to open her mouth to breathe cause she'll drown . . . well . . . I'd like to think I'll one day change my mind about myself, and kind of like myself again, maybe have better dreams."

Dave Cato, his craggy face breaking into a mischievous grin is in the moment now. He must just briefly not be thinking of his wife. He's thinking of me and finally picks up his previously abandoned Coke, raises it in the air and offers, "Well, I like you, Ranger Billie. I like how you lit a fire under me." *Does he know?*

"Here's to you and here's to me and if we chance should disagree, here's to me. Ha!"

I correct him. "I think that's 'to hell with you and here's to me.'" *So what if he suspects me. I appreciate the gesture, Dave Cato's rescue.*

"I know. I was just being easy on you. See, you had to tack that *hell with you* on there cause that's where you're at right now."

"I'm in hell?"

"Yup. You can't see the glass half full cause you're half empty. You need to be feeling good about something. And here's something."

"Tell me what it is; I need to hear it."

"I'm going to move my wife to a better facility, and I'm going to do it because of what you shared. Alice's life is in decline, but maybe she can be declining in that culture of caring you're talking about. As far as I'm concerned, you've saved her, and by extension, me."

In fact I do feel better. Lifted up instead of pulled down, Dave's full endorsement. The reconstruction of Ranger Billie.

"Okay, then. Let me try a toast. *The fleeting clouds may kiss the sky. The flowers may kiss the butterfly. The spring wine may kiss the glass, and you, dear friend,* ... Ha ha."

I down my Coke, raise the can into the air, "Dave Cato, kindred spirit, we count ourselves among the walking wounded, our club an exclusive and private fraternity."

"And no one is lining up to get in!" Dave chimes in. Then he leans forward, close to my face. "We may be the walking wounded but I have enough scars to know that wounds heal." It's almost an admonishment.

Suddenly infused with a new energy, from where I can't imagine, he rises, raises his can of coke and offers, "May all our wounds heal, and may we live long, but not tooooo long," finger pointing upward, cautionary. His meaning needs no explaining to me.

CHAPTER 12

LEGACY FOREST

It's a fall Friday, and the main beach house parking lot is packed which means the facility has been reserved for an engagement, maybe a  wedding; people have them even on Fridays nowadays. Maybe a retirement party or an anniversary.

The structure's two-story window towers over the beach and provides a view of the lake all the way across to the west end. An enormous floor-to-ceiling stone fireplace occupies the opposite wall of this building and, unlike the shelter on the park's north end, is completely walled in and heated; it's a popular and affordable space for a large gathering.

The only ranger problem it poses is parking. Patrons have to pay a parking fee. Sometimes families arrange to prepay parking and ask the attendant or ranger to dispense car permits as the guests drive in. Or after guests come in, the ranger or the park foreman contacts the host family member, gets his count of guests and then the county office bills for parking. If all the cars have permits on their windshields, I don't have to ruin a party by writing parking tickets.

Inside the park office, the foreman has just prepared my paperwork, a copy of the beach house registration agreement. He hands it to me as I walk in the door.

"Funeral today, Billie," and he leaves his office.

A funeral at the park is unusual but not unheard of. I glance first at the hours; it's for afternoon use, a visitation until 4 p.m. followed by a memorial service. The name of the party: Cato family. *Uh-oh.* Contact person: Robert Cato. *Dave's son?* I look out the window to see the foreman drive to the beach house. He'll check out accommodations, registrant, and parking arrangements before he turns the park over to me.

It could be Alice's funeral. Dave had been talking about a service for her. Or it could be Dave's. He did collapse not long ago, and his care-giving duties have taken a lot out him. Either way, I'm feeling uneasy.

I'm in the Silverado beginning rounds in the park when the foreman radios that the funeral attendees all have permits for their cars. "All you need to do is check the facility and lock up after they leave," he reminds me.

"Just one more thing before you 10-42," I say. "Who died?"

"Dave Cato, the old guy who wore a Panama hat."

. . . .

Some people's attachment to the park is deep. They purchase a tree for planting in Fox Brook's Legacy Forest to commemorate a birth, a wedding, a graduation or to memorialize a lost loved one. Each tree has a connection and a story. But many park  visitors never see these natural monuments to a human life because the Legacy Forest is situated in a section lower than the rest of the terrain and far away from the beach. The bike and walking path that follows the edge of the 22-acre quarry doesn't skirt the forest.

Fox Brook is predominately wetland, 138 acres of wetland, and The Legacy Forest is part of it. In summer, the only moisture-laden part of the park patrons want is the lake. Although the city of Brookfield treats the area wetlands for mosquitoes and the park has installed bat houses to attract mosquito-eating creatures of the night, mosquitoes still appear when conditions are right and park patrons try to avoid them. In season, park workers mow loops through the wild grasses and native plant communities of the Legacy Forest so visitors can amble from tree to tree or sit on a wooden bench to contemplate within view of the meandering pathway.

In winter, The Legacy Forest and neighboring wetlands are stark, the trees barren of leaves and the grey-brown land flattened by icy snow, but the familiar passageway through the trees is still visible. It is not plowed in the winter, but animals like a path of least resistance in their snowy travels, so they keep the path tamped down. And in winter, off duty, I enjoy following the wildlife through what seem like hallowed cemetery grounds.

. . . .

I remember circumnavigating the lake on the paved bike and pedestrian path one brisk December day; a man walking his golden retriever remarked to me, "I don't know which season of the park I like better-winter with all its peaceful silence, or summer with all the happy sounds of kids on the beach."

"Today, I'm leaning slightly toward winter," I say. The dog isn't leashed and I don't have to do anything about it. Today I am park patron not park ranger.

I continue past the shelter on the north side and then down into the Legacy Forest. Snow covers the wetland-looks like a giant tract of winter meadow, only short tufts of growth covered in fresh white snow. Leafless specimens of birch, oak, honey locust, ash, maple and linden comprise the young forest.

There are prints of birds and animal traffic. I have met on this path no fewer than two skunks, one young opossum, a porcupine, a coyote with a dead bunny hanging from its mouth, wild turkeys, squirrels and chipmunks. Drops of bright red in the snow concern me now; I know they're blood. The deer prints don't follow the pattern a typical deer on the move makes. *Looks like one hoof has been dragging.* I follow the trail past young trees, each a reminder of someone who was loved. The Legacy Trail ends, but the path used by animals continues, in this case to the edge of Gateway Commerce Center at the far western edge of the park.

A bird feeder sits on top of a pole behind the automotive supplies building. Sometimes a hawk is perched on a rain gutter or on the top of a leafless tree, watching silently, waiting for a careless sparrow or a foraging mouse in the grass beneath the feeder. Then it will swoop down, quiet and lethal, Nature's stealth bomber. I have to smile. Dave Cato had said, "They have to eat, too."

But today, I spot the source of the blood trail, an injured deer awkwardly stretching its neck downward to feed on bird seed that has spilled onto the ground. One of the doe's rear legs is fractured, bone broken through skin.

I stand at quiet attention behind a tree line, but the deer, nostrils taking in my scent, ears turned to my direction, senses human presence; she's either too hungry or too weak to flee.

I open my cell phone and quietly back away. First the police. They can't do anything but give me the number of the Elmbrook Humane Society. I dial the number and in hushed tones explain the deer predicament. They cannot send someone unless the deer is down. If the deer is standing, it has a chance of surviving on its own the woman on the phone explains. But because I can see the rawness of the wound, bone broken clear through, and bleeding that hasn't stopped, I don't share the humane society's optimism.

. . . .

Later that winter, I saw the deer at the same feeder. It seemed to have developed a feeding routine probably encouraged by sympathetic Gateway workers keeping bird feeders full, maybe supplanting with food on the ground.

About a half mile from this spot and near the entrance to Fox Brook Park, a bow hunting target range had been embellished with a homemade wooden silhouette of a deer leaned up against a bale of hay. A red circle covers the part of the target the hunter is supposed to hit, the heart, for what's called the "clean kill."

I don't know if it's for spite or by coincidence, but the injured deer did not avoid the target range. It actually bedded down in a tree line that bordered the property, tucked its three good legs under itself as darkness fell, about 5 p.m. on days walkers saw her; then by morning, according to neighbors, gone, just impressions in the snow. But as the days lengthened and winter began finally to abate, each time I saw the deer grazing on spilled bird feed, its fracture seemed less gruesome, and it could hobble along on three legs. Before winter turned to spring, what had been bones broken through raw flesh morphed into a bulbous cluster of calcium and scar tissue which stiffened the deer's stride and gave it an awkward gait, more of a rudder than a fourth leg, but it had survived, muddled through the winter, stared down the deer target and ran on all fours. It did heal.

I recall telling the story to Dave Cato who surprised me, actually disappointed me, with his absence of surprise . . .

"I have enough scars to know that wounds heal, told you that before," and then he changed the subject. "You know what I'm going to have the minister read at my wife's funeral?"

"You know that she's dying soon?"

"No, but I want to be prepared. It's the 23rd Psalm, the one about going through the shadow of the valley of death," he said.

"What made you want to tell me about that right now?"

"You just told me about the deer and the Legacy Forest. It's related."

"And I don't know how so you're going to tell me?"

"Okay, it goes like this . . .

'The Twenty-Third Psalm

'The Lord is my shepherd; I shall not want.
He maketh me to lie down in green pastures:'"

Impatient because he summarily dismissed my story and expected attention paid his, I implore, "Dave, I do know the psalm."

"But listen especially to the end.

'He leadeth me beside the still waters.
He restoreth my soul: He leadeth me in the paths of
righteousness
for His name's sake.
Yea, though I walk through the valley of the shadow of death,
I fear no evil:
For though art with me . . .'

I mean it doesn't say you go *into* the valley of death. It says *through*. That means you come out the other side. That means life."

"Man, Dave, you are deep, but you have a point."

"A point? It's more than a point, even if you aren't religious, you have to admit, the deer went through something, not around, or under; it went right on through and came out alive whole, if just a little gimpy."

He *had* listened to my story. "Okay, I'll give you this. My path to seeing the deer ordeal was upon going though the Legacy Forest. It's something you do go down into, not exactly a valley, but it's after passing through that I saw the doe. So that means what?"

Dave isn't sure if I'm mocking him or not, but he gives me the benefit of *his* doubt and continues. "It's a metaphor for life after death, right here in the park. If you don't see that, it's only because you're blind. Your loss."

"I concede, I did not believe the deer would survive. So maybe it's a magical place, Dave, or a place where miracles happen. At first I thought the deer was a miracle, but maybe it's the whole place."

"It's a spiritual place, Ranger Billie. All of nature is like that."

"I know better than to argue with you."

"Good," he mutters and nods his head. "My brain is tired."

"Yes, good. Here you are in a situation, with your wife's Alzheimer's and all. I know how grueling that is. You must be tired, period. Doesn't seem to get you down in spirits, though."

Dave gets up from the park bench and pulls up his loose trousers. He's lost weight. "Don't analyze that. Just remember that life finds a way."

"But still, we all die," I say to his back. "I don't want to make you sad, but your wife will die, too."

Dave turns around, not missing a beat, "And I'm getting ready for that now. The last thing I will do for her, and I'm preparing to now, because it is such an important and loving act, is let her go."

And just like that, he's on his way. *He's standing up and going through*, I thought. Back to the nursing home, with his faith and his optimism and his wife and her Alzheimer's . . .

. . . .

After the funeral, I held my own vigil for Dave Cato. I drove to the spot where he had covertly released a chipmunk into the park just before I met him, under a tree so it would  have nuts and near the water so it could drink. Seated now at the picnic bench under which the no-kill trap once sat, I made my evening log entry.

. . . .

RANGER LOG

Date: *Oct. 21*

Time: *7 p.m.*

Main shelter, funeral service. Parking permits on cars, complete compliance . . .

. . . .

But the writing didn't come easily, so I walked to the bench which faces the path through The Legacy Forest.

There I marveled at how letting go became Dave Cato's final act of love, how The Legacy Forest itself colored his world and how his world included his sons . . .

After the service, I invited myself to Dave's funeral gathering. I was on duty as a ranger, in uniform, too. I could have appeared to check on the facility, the main beach house, but I really wanted to be part of the celebration of Dave Cato's life, at least to pay my respects. I introduced myself as a ranger and a friend of the deceased and offered a handshake to a young man who looked remarkably like his father.

"I'm Robert, one of his sons. It's nice to meet you. My dad loved this park. That's why the funeral is here. Used to bring Alice here, too."

"He did, yes, and I met your mother on several occasions."

"You met Alice? She wasn't my mother, though. Alice is my dad's second wife. My mother died."

He looked down at his feet, thinking. About his mother? About his father? About his inheritance? I don't know, but he's wearing black cowboy boots and trying to rub a scuff mark off the left one with the toe of the right one. *Alice was his stepmother.* "Then you know about the Alzheimer's," he said in a lowered tone as though it were some kind of secret. "We didn't tell her he died. I don't think we will."

"Those decisions are hard. He used to visit her every day. Will she wonder why he isn't coming?"

He's shuffling his feet again now, but he's looking at me. "I don't know if she remembers he visits her every day. It's hard to say. It might be hard for her to know he died."

"Did she know him? I mean did she still recognize him?"

He's looking around now, maybe for other guests, maybe tiring of this conversation. "Dad thought she did, but Dad was kind of fanatical about the whole thing, maybe a little in denial. My brother and I think he was having a hard time letting go, always complaining about her care and stuff."

"Do you think she's getting good care?"

Now it's his black-booted feet he's watching again. Maybe he wants his feet to take him away. Maybe he's feeling interrogated. "Well, it's a *skilled care* facility. And they always treat her kindly when I'm there," he finally blurted.

I picked up some defensiveness, maybe some condescension, too. "And when is that? And how is the care when you're not there?" I persisted.

That I wasn't at this memorial service just to pay my respects was an epiphany for Robert.

"Excuse me," he offered, gave me his back and clomped off in his disrespectful dirty black cowpoke boots ...

Outside, I met the other son, David II, who had exited to smoke a cigarette. From him I learned that Dave Cato was a type 1 diabetic who hadn't been monitoring his blood sugar or eating as directed, and they doubted he was taking his medication correctly. David believed his father was "losing it" himself and that his collapse in the park was health related, not necessarily heat related. But this time I tried to stay clear of nursing home issues.

"Your dad served in Nam? That was my generation's war."

"Yes, he was a veteran, decorated. He got two purple hearts, too. He gave one to me and one to my brother. My impression was he didn't want them in his possession. He wasn't proud of them."

This son is lighting another cigarette, but at least he's looking at me instead of his boots as he speaks. I add, "He didn't like hunting, didn't like killing, he told me. Actually, that was one of the first things he ever told me about himself."

"He was anti war. He told us living well is all about building. War is all about destruction."

"He told me things like that, like how we didn't need the War of Independence; we could have been a great big United Kingdom and been spared useless loss of life ..." but now David is looking around like his brother did, probably wanting this funeral business over with. Or maybe his dad's war views were a source of friction. I changed course. "He'd make profound observations, sometimes kind of provocative. But he had faith, religious faith, in Jesus." Then I described Dave's favorite CNA Tuma, the "builder." But I'd lost eye contact again. The young David did not share his father's pacifist outlook or my enthusiasm for Tuma, and he'd fixated on the previous comment about war and destruction.

"Yeah, well, my dad never could get that sometimes war is the only alternative."

"But he went to Nam anyway."

"Of course! You can't be a Cato male in our family and not serve your country when called, and he was called."

"The lottery draft-his number came up?"

"Yes."

"Now there is no draft—just a volunteer army. So you and your brother, did you volunteer and serve in the military, too?"

He looked at me queerly, took a long draw of his cigarette, but he didn't give me his back like his brother did. "I would serve *if called*." Then his back. The confrontation-avoiding sons had not inherited their father's convictions or his charming personality, and I'm finding once again that an aggressive cross-examination doesn't earn points at a funeral.

And the new details about Dave raised more questions than they answered.

Did Dave Cato do all that planning because he expected not to live long? He wanted the value of his estate going right to Alice and the new nursing home. Did he expect his sons to oppose the plan? And did he arrange, with a lawyer, to have his property sold and Alice admitted to CompassionCare Home?

Some of my questions were answered later when Kruege Attorney at Law called. Dave Cato had updated his will. He had also recently set up a trust. His lake property was in the trust and the executor of the trust, a friend (not one of his sons) was directed to sell the lake property and use the funds to support Alice's care in CompassionCare Home. The trust also named an advocate for overseeing Alice's transition into the home. The advocate was Ranger Billie of Fox Brook Park.

Of course the sons took issue with the plan, but it was legally locked up tight. The sons had commiserated with each other, " . . . he's feeble . . . in denial . . . and resisting letting her go." They had eyes but they did not see; that's how Dave might put it. If I were to give my impressions of the Cato sons, I might say, "*They* were feeble, *they* were in denial, and they were *in a hurry to let their stepmother go.*"

SEASON THREE

2008

CHAPTER 13

WORLD AT WAR AND HOLY MAN

Alice's dining room at CompassionCare Home is embellished with white, linen-covered tables, fresh flowers, lots of windows, a fireplace on one end, huge fish tank on the other, and plenty of staff. Sometimes I'm there in my ranger uniform. I pull up a chair to Alice's table and introduce myself to Alice's tablemates as I have done many times. "I'm Ranger Billie." They expect a ranger story or two, but I believe they'd be happy just enjoying the presence of someone "from the outside" even if all the presence did was sit with them. After repeating pleasantries and exchanging smiles, I direct my attention to Alice who is eating her dessert first.

"Would you like to hear the story *The Man in the Panama Hat* again?"

Alice is attentive, but not answering. She's probably not clear what the question was. People with Alzheimer's can hear, but some of the message gets lost during processing of language. Sometimes well intentioned nurses and nurse aides repeat the question only a lot louder. More confusion for the patient. Alice may only recall *hat* or *Panama hat*. Or she may be thinking, "*Again* what?" She may even say, "My mind is blank," and she won't be speaking metaphorically.

"Alice. Here is a picture of Dave."

Alice looks at the picture. "I don't remember him."

"Alice, I'll tell you a story. It will help you remember."

"Okay. Do you have a car?"

"Yes."

"Let's get out of here."

"Let me tell you a story first."

Sometimes Alice has to be redirected, but she does like stories and I can tell her the same ones; annoyance at repetition isn't an issue with Alice.

Alzheimer's patients can't recall all of a multiple part question, tend to remember the last word or words, so I try to place the most important word at the end of the question. "Alice, which stories do you like the most?" becomes "Alice, did you like the story of the man with the straw hat?"

She usually says either, "Yes," or, "I loved the man in the straw hat," and I don't know if she means the story or *the man*.

. . . .

Other days, Alice's many lonely hours are eased by the presence of the summer girl I met during the white wedding of the previous year. She's really not a "girl"; she's an almost 18-year-old single woman now who would be giving birth soon.

Dave Cato's planning for his wife included financing the presence of an advocate in her life. To comply, I did oversee her admission and transition into CompassionCare Home as Dave Cato's plan had directed, but primary caregiving and advocacy for an Alzheimer's patient is an assignment for someone who hadn't already just about burned out. By the time Dave died, Tuma had already left Riversite. He had been going to school, completing a degree, and was now a registered nurse working in Oregon. Someone's gain but Riversite's loss and Alice's loss, too. Dave had directed me to pay Tuma to care for Alice as her own private CNA; he offered to compensate him generously. Instead, I offered part time employment to Fox Brook's summer girl as Alice's sitter. Some churches and organizations for elder support provide volunteers to "sit with" people like Alice, to be a compassionate presence (compassion in the classic sense, to "be with" the sufferer) in the lives of those who have been largely abandoned. In this role, they relieve loneliness as well as become eyes that can observe care and memories that can provide details. Unlike the wards in their care, "sitters" are not afraid to report inadequate care or in worse cases, abuse. They can observe good and bad care.

The girl is taking a home schooling option for her senior year and is going along with her parents' insistence that she attend college while living at home. The "sitting" job is in fact a refuge for her. Alice is not combative. She can be rather catatonic, but she enjoys someone sitting with her. Benefits for the girl: She gets a break from studying and from her parents, she's being paid by Dave Cato in abstentia, the fact of her baby is not questioned or judged, and she can prattle away about her plans, her problems, her baby, etc. in complete confidence because Alice isn't going to remember. She can tell Alice *everything*.

. . . .

An aide checks the contents of Alice's styrofoam water cup and brushes past the girl. "Is that an engagement ring on your left hand?"

"Yes, it is."

"So you're going to marry the father of your baby?"

"No." She does not look at the questioner.

"Oh. Well, it's none of my business," but she waits for an explanation. There being none, she persists, "Congratulations, anyway."

"Thank you." But she doesn't elaborate and the girl expects the aide is speculating whether the young mother is really engaged at all . . .

. . . .

"Alice, that woman is all bent out of shape cause I'm not telling her about my situation. It's none of her business, you know. I don't mind telling you, though. Would you like to know about her, my baby?" She pats her bulging stomach and looks for a response from Alice. Alice smiles.

"The father has red hair; he dyed it other colors, too, and made it spiky." She lifts her hair in demonstration and Alice's eyes follow her motions. "But it is really red, so maybe I'll have a red-headed little girl."

Alice seems engaged, so she continues, "Plus, he was always getting into trouble. Not a good student, not because he was dumb, though. He was super smart and they put him in classes for the gifted and talented, but he thought all of that was pretty dumb, too. He just gave the teachers a hard time till he got kicked out of classes. He would tell them things like, 'You're problem is you can't control your class.' Teachers just love a kid like that—NOT!" she laughs and Alice's smile widens.

"I thought he was totally bizarre, not anyone I wanted to have anything to do with. And here I am with this baby bump."

Alice giggles when she hears "baby bump" and sees the girl tenderly pat her stomach.

"The thing that made me fall kind of totally for him was what happened in the cafeteria one day when a retarded, well not really retarded, but kind of disabled kid that everybody liked came into the room; he was in a wheelchair. He used to be able to walk, but he got worse and had to use the chair which he hated. I guess he was embarrassed by it. Anyway, he wheeled into the cafeteria, and this big jerk loser kept sticking his metal ruler into the spokes of the chair wheels so the kid couldn't maneuver, but he couldn't figure out why cause he couldn't see what the guy was doing behind him—except he was laughing at him. Some kids were yelling at the bully to stop it, and the yelling just confused the kid in the chair. His face, the disabled kid's face, was getting redder and redder, and then my boyfriend, well, he wasn't my boyfriend yet, but he just jumped right over a cafeteria table and kids' trays and food went flying and stuff, and he grabbed that heckler jerk by the neck and threw him against the wall. He was like batman without the cape. He probably should have stopped then, but he didn't; he pounded that kid til he cried. No one tried to stop him til the teachers hauled him away. He got suspended. I thought he was awesome. I couldn't stop thinking about him and how he wouldn't stand for that kid being ridiculed, and how he wasn't afraid of getting into trouble himself. Don't you think he was kind of heroic?"

"Are we related?" Alice asks.

A little deflated at having her drama not given its due, she answers, "No, I'm just a friend."

"Oh, I thought you were my niece or something."

"No, but we're like family. We spend a lot of time together."

"I know! And I so enjoy your visits. They don't visit me anymore."

"They?"

"Who?"

130

"Who doesn't visit you anymore?"

"Nobody."

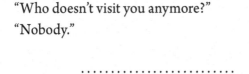

Because the girl is kind, she's perfect for the job. Even her attraction to the young man known as the menace of Fox Brook Park was due to an act of kindness she observed, the rescue of a handicapped kid. She didn't like seeing abuse or ridicule; she liked the rescue. From her point of view, the strength is kindness. I saw kindness extended to students in the classroom. It sometimes was rewarded with unruly behavior, kindness sometimes interpreted wrongly as weakness. Well, that's immature kids for you. So in a sense, in spite of the trouble this girl finds herself in, she has maturity of a sort that really matters in this nursing home. She is sensitive to Alice's disease.

Now she knows this conversation isn't going to lead Alice to a pleasant place, so she redirects her.

"I went to his graduation party. His parents were home, but they weren't around much. I went with him to a bedroom; everybody had been drinking. And that's how this happened." She points to her belly. "Do you think I'm bad?"

Alice blurts, "The world is at war; arm yourself!"

The girl turns on Alice's television, "Let's watch the Sandra Lee cooking show. I'll turn it on."

. . . .

When I talk with the girl, she tells me what she's learned about Alzheimer's. People with Alzheimer's don't necessarily verbalize their needs, can't clearly communicate pain, for example. The aides at CompassionCare have been trained in nonverbal pain indicators, and the girl has observed; she's a quick study. She knows if Alice becomes agitated after dinner, that means she's uncomfortable and needs to be toileted. Alice's dentures used to float in her mouth and Alice clicked them. Her aides at Riversite attributed that behavior to senility. A dentist established that it was pain. Alice's gums, under the dentures, had ulcerated. She needed treatment. Since Alzheimer's patients' not being able to articulate makes them doubly susceptible to being undertreated for pain or infection.

The girl offers Alice ice water, puts the cup in her hands. But, at the moment, Alice seems content. Sandra Lee is on the TV screen. She's pretty, she uses simple expressions like, "This is great . . . This is easy . . . This is beautiful," and Alice is smiling. When Sandra Lee's cooking program ends, the girl offers to entertain Alice with a letter she has received.

But an intercom message intercedes, "Alice, report to the nurse's station for a phone call." There is a nurse named Alice, and the call is probably a family member checking on a resident, but Alice-the-resident hears her name and wheels herself through the doorway. An aide in the hall says, "It's not for you, Alice," but doesn't obstruct her passage. Alice is on a mission because a voice of authority told her to report to the nurse's station.

"She'll get halfway to or all the way to the nurse's station and then she'll not be sure what she's doing there and will make her way back, or I'll go get her," the aide explains to the girl in Alice's room.

"Good. I was just getting ready to read to her."

In the hallway, Alice-the-resident is intercepted by Alice-the-nurse who wheels the former back to her "sitter" who is more than anxious to disengage from the prying aide.

"Alice, I have a letter here. Do you know who we're at war with? Wait. We're at war in Afghanistan. Who is the enemy?"

"I'll have to study up on that." Alice, like other Alzheimer's patients, has learned to weasel around a task that requires memory. She doesn't admit, "I don't know." It's as though the cognition to deflect has compensated for the loss of cognition to remember.

"Well, we are fighting militant Islamic extremists in Afghanistan," and she begins to read when Alice's face brightens like a light switch has just turned on in her head. She interrupts, "The world is at war; arm yourself."

But the girl unfolds the letter and begins to read, "In training at Camp Lejeune, N.C., I learned to suffer; that's what they want you to do. Sniper school is designed to push you to your limits. They have to know who will hold up under pressure, and they want to find out before deployment. But I had plenty of experience in the misery department before I even got here and that brings me to my dad. He practically renamed me 'stubborn bastard.' He thought he was putting me down, but over here, we don't show emotion, so stubborn bastard works for me. Only they call it 'heart.' It's like a will to succeed and it's not something that can be taught. Either you have it or you don't. I already screwed up a lot at home, as you know, but I'm not screwing up this . . ."

Now a wandering resident has wheeled himself into Alice's room and he's headed toward her bathroom. He probably needs to be toileted and isn't waiting for help. Alice is becoming agitated. She grimaces. "There's a man in my room," she protests. Alice could turn on her call light if she could remember she has one, but the girl pushes it for her. At Riversite, Alice might have waited a long time for help, but here at CompassionCare the response to her call light is swift. For that Dave Cato's estate pays about $10,000 a month plus an endowment fee. A caregiver wheels the wayward old man out of her room. Alice parks herself in her doorway as a barricade to further encroachment, and the girl knows the letter reading will have to wait. Alice is on point.

The writer of the letter, the father of the girl's baby, entered Second Marine Division on Camp Lejeune, North Carolina to become Hunter of Gunmen (HOG). Goal: Special Forces Marine, Marine Special Operations Battalion (MSOB). That's Not Marine Sons of Bitches as is mistakenly assumed. The menace at Fox Brook Park became a military man, a "hunter," a U.S. Marine sniper.

No *fobbit* job, no Forward Operating Base assignment. This Marine wanted a combat mission.

. . . .

And the Marine menace is on my mind today as my a.m. shift at Fox Brook Park approaches. I pull into the entrance and pass the attendant's booth—no one there yet. Ahead of me a  teenage boy is pulling at the rigging of the flag staff. *Is he a seasonal employee doing custodial work or is he a new park menace?* My cell phone rings.

"Billie, this is Sherlock."

"Merlin? You must have found something really big!"

Merlin the Metal Man says, "I never seen anything like it. You told me to call you any time if I found something about that biker, remember? Why don't you drive right on over to the park. Meet me and the foreman at the office."

"Wait. What did you find out? I can't stand suspense."

"Nope. You gotta see it."

. . . .

The Silverado is parked outside and leaning against it are an agitated Merlin and the foreman's assistant. Grateful for inclusion over the find, I pull in a little too enthusiastically and have to slam hard on the brakes to avoid hitting the foreman who has just appeared from behind the truck with his palms out, "Whoa."

On the rustic picnic bench which the ranger vehicle has obscured, a brown tarp-covered bundle contains whatever has become the source of jubilance. The foreman takes a draw of his Chesterfield Light and exhales smoke though grinning lips. He points to the main beach house. "Billie, remember the bicycle menace?"

Of course I remember the infamous menace, bully son of a bully, and reckless racer, who joined the Marines after he turned 18, just after becoming a true horny toad. *They need a few good men, but compassion and empathy are not prerequisites.* "Who could forget?"

"Well, he reformed."

The foreman then pieces together for his assistant, Merlin the Metal Man, and me, the story of the metamorphosis of the menace of Fox Brook Park. On a tour in Afghanistan, be was befriended by a Baptist chaplain who somehow hooked him on Jesus. The menace sent the park foreman a Bible and a letter asking for his forgiveness. On the inside cover, he inscribed an official apology for all his misbehaviors and for stealing park property. He said he buried it all in the park one night before he shipped out, fully intending to one day return and continue his rebel acts. With the help of Merlin and his metal detector, the box of stolen goods was recovered and now sat atop the park office picnic table. The treasures included a life guard bull horn, several rolls of quarters probably snatched from the concession stand when the menace managed to infiltrate the booth, a ranger flashlight, a bicycle helmet and other nonlethal items, but more unsettling, it did include two Glock semi-automatic pistols and bullets. What vendetta the menace had planned for his return is subject to conjecture, but discovering the contraband made this Fox Brook foursome grateful for the intercession of a chaplain. The holy terror of Fox Brook Park was now just holy.

"There's one more thing, Billie. There's this wallet; it's got Dave Cato's ID in it. You know anything about that?"

The wallet. There never was an explanation for the missing wallet. Dave's sons said their father was forgetful; he was. *But maybe the menace did assault and rob the man in the straw hat. Or maybe Dave Cato did drop or leave his wallet somewhere and the menace lifted it. He didn't mention it in his apology or confession . . . Let this one go.*

I say, "No, I don't know anything about that."

Merlin chimes in, "I think the menace called 911 the day Dave Cato collapsed."

I pick up the bull horn, recall its illicit use, then inspect the ranger high powered LED flashlight and wonder how he got it; mine was always attached to my belt. There's an additional flashlight in the cab with the first aid kit and the defibrillator, but I always left the Silverado locked. Maybe another ranger left it unlocked during a foot patrol? But the guns and ammo. He didn't get those from the park and for whose demise were they assembled here?

Now I consider Merlin's remark. "What makes you think he called 911? He wasn't reformed then."

"No, not reformed. But he was struggling. He was suffering."

"You sound kind of Buddhist. Buddhists think everyone is suffering."

"Everyone *is* suffering."

I consider that. *Certainly all of us want our suffering relieved. The menace found a way.*

"Does he say when his tour is up?" I ask the foreman.

"He doesn't. But his tour *is* up. He was killed in Afghanistan yesterday."

The proverbial jaw drop. *My stomach, that shudder, that roil, it's always the same when the door's been slammed on someone's life with such finality. The permanent end to my brother, my father, my friend, then my mother; it's immobilizing and it never ends. The menace wasn't a loved one. Was he? Or did I have important business with him that could not be transacted now?*

The foreman faces me and hands over Dave Cato's wallet. The dizziness is dispelled. "Do you want to take this to Dave Cato's wife? It's got family pictures in it."

I numbly accept the weathered remnant, finger it.

"Okay. She like pictures ... but just a minute. Did ... did the menace say anything about me in his letter to you?"

"No. I'm the one he thought was the enemy. Although he probably would have popped whoever threw his bike into the bog."

But, dropping onto the bench seat and staring into the menace's cache, I cannot conceal my disappointment.

"It's just that I sent him a letter, a sort of apology of my own. Now I don't know if he even got it."

"You sent *him* an apology?

"Yup. Long story."

"See, everybody *is* suffering," Merlin observed aloud.

. . . .

The young park employee fiddling with the rigging got the flag lowered as the foreman probably ordered. It's flying at half staff for the menace of Fox Brook Park. No doubt he could have out terrorized any Taliban fighter, made himself invisible, taken that knockout shot, but against an IED, he had few defensive resources. *Afghanistan was the menace's Waterloo, but he would say, "It was also my Salvation."*

SEASON FOUR

2009

CHAPTER 14

WEDDING

"We picked red maple in honor of your dad's red hair." That's what I tell the frowning, but not crying, 17-month-old whom I've just carried into The Legacy Forest. She fingers the few crisp leaves that haven't yet given way to fall. They crumple in her hands like little potato chips, and she presses them to her lips.

"No, no," I admonish and wipe leaf bits away from the little mouth. This sends her hands into a flurry of movement; she's trying to sign to me.

"I'm sorry. All I can do is talk. I don't know signing." She pulls sunglasses away from my face and smiles at her wide-eyed self reflected in the lenses. With one hand exploring sunglasses and the other fingering my badge, Allie will be occupied long enough to endure my homily.

"Today your mother is marrying the legendary dog whisperer of Fox Brook Park. He's an extraordinary young man, and you will be calling him Daddy. But someday, I will tell you your biological dad's story. I would like to, anyway. Someone should tell you. Here at Fox Brook Park, before he shipped out, he was incubating or percolating or something, a work in progress and a great work at that, I believe. But that is for another day.

Today you will hear the story of the world in general because you need to be spoken to, with all due respect to your deaf-mute adoptive father. I will narrate this story in little nuggets, little essences. My high school students might have paid attention if history class had been this short:

History 101

Ch. 1: There was a time when Man thought he and his earth were the center of the known universe, kind of a popular but arrogant notion; then a rogue scientist came along and debunked that. First Galileo was laughed at and ridiculed. Later his truth-telling life was threatened. I would have let him hide in my house. The Catholic Church then got kind of Talibanish about it. But eventually the truth of his theories won over critics. Man and his earth are spinning around the sun. Everyone, almost everyone, except about twenty per cent of Russians, is on board with Galileo now. What do you think?"

"Gaaagh. Goooo." She pulls at the badge but it's securely attached.

"I agree. It's pretty neat. Ch. 2: Man also thought he was given special dominion and created separately from other living things, kind of a conceited idea; then someone named Darwin came along and refuted that. Like Galileo, he was laughed at and ridiculed. Some people are still mad at him and insist on the creation stories of their religions to explain the origins of Man. I think those stories can be compatible with science but not everyone agrees. As you grow up, you will find that not everyone agrees on just about everything. But most concur now that Man is a primate, evolved from other primates, and he doesn't have any more control over his earth than the wind or the willow has." I smile at the girl and kiss her head. "Are you following this?"

"Gwiiiii gaaa guh!"

"Yes, indeed! Isn't history fun! Ch. 3: Man thought, next, at least of his own mind he had control; then an independent thinker came along and nixed that. Freud theorized a conscious and subconscious mind, the subconscious not directed by the conscious. He was shunned at first; now his works are seminal. By seminal, I mean who's arguing now?"

The little red head is leaning forward now, closing her eyes.

"I was a great tranquilizer for my high school students, too!" The pedagogy continues. "General Application for the Present: What history teaches us is that we're only part of the universe, but not front and center and not in control. And you know, by extension, we are not the center of even our own universes. I don't know that we should be anyway, that we should operate like nobody else is important. What happens to humility if you think you're the center of your universe? Bullies are the center of their universes!"

A chipmunk scurries across the path in front my feet, and I wonder if it's a relation of the creatures Dave Cato used to catch and release. Then I turn back to the little redhead, beautiful in repose, tiny lips slightly open, breathing quietly. I take a closer look, make sure she *is* breathing.

Once assured of respiration, I continue, "Personal Application: I'm especially interested in Ch. 3, the mind part because I almost lost mine in recent years, stuck in a situation; call it grief. Hope you don't have much of that in your life. But you'll have some—no getting around that if you're going to be alive. There's a pathology to grief— anger being an unwelcome component—and recovery has accepted pathways: talk therapy, drug therapy, the old fashioned passage-of-time therapy, even 'just get over it' therapy. There's another one, though. Call it rogue if you will, but don't laugh. I'm finding my cure right now, right here. The man in the straw hat thinks . . . *thought* . . . it's here," I survey The Legacy Forest, "in this park."

But I may just as well have been singing a lullaby. The little red head is sleeping, her small fingers still wrapped around the sheriff's badge over the shirt pocket, her head cradled her in the crook of my right arm.

Meanwhile, several wedding guests seeing Fox Brook Park for the first time approach me.

"It's such a treasure. How could I live nearby and never know it's here?" a Brookfield resident squeals.

"Well, you don't see the lake from the road or from the turn into the park. You know how people are; if they can't see something, it's not there." *Like disbelievers*. Dave Cato would second that thought and add something like, "People don't believe because they're blind to what's right in front of them. Their loss."

Others are curious about where the sand on the beach comes from, are there lots for sale in the area, what was here before the park, etc. I tell them about the Potawatomie Indians, their burials and celebrations; kids love to hear about the Indians eating dogs, not about the Fox River. And, no it's not a pond. Pond—you can walk across and be breathing all the way to the other side. Lake, you sink or swim. Fox Brook's lake is as deep as 30 feet. It was a stone quarry. It's used for scuba diving lessons now. It has had a drowning. Such is not the history of a "pond."

I can see now the dog whisperer, dressed in a white tuxedo, walking toward the shelter in a large group that includes 17 kids—all those grandchildren. Even his lopsided dog, elegantly clad in a dog tux, is participating. His task, on signal from his master, "Fetch the bouquet out of the bride's hands and deliver it to the single bridesmaid before the couple exchange vows, before they each *sign* their vows."

I sense someone tall, someone who casts a long shadow coming up behind me. It's my sup. He sidles toward the park bench, and he doesn't look glad to see me. "You told me you'd never see that girl again," and nods toward the bride.

"Shhhhh. The kid fell asleep. I didn't think I would see the girl again. But she came back to the park. She'd visit Alice at the nursing home, and then she'd come to the park and tell me about it. Then after she had the baby, she'd come to the park and wheel her around in a stroller."

"And then she met the guy here?"

"Yeah, they just gravitated to one another."

"Maybe with a little help from someone?"

"Yes, I had something to do with it. Let me explain. Look at the groom. See how he resembles that Nero actor who was Italian in real life but the French knight Lancelot in *Camelot*?"

The sup's face is a blank. "You mean *Spamalot*?"

"No, no, no! *Camelot*! Remember, the musical movie? *He's older than me so he should remember.* Rex Harris was King Arthur, Vanessa Redgrave was Gwenivere, and Franco Nero was Lancelot," I insist. "He was enormously conceited, handsome and sang *C'est moi*, the song about the wonderfulness of himself. Look at the groom. See the resemblance?"

"But he can't sing."

"You're hopeless! Gwenivere falls in love with Lancelot when he cries, not when he sings. This bride doesn't care about *her* shining knight's voice either."

"Gwen was the king's queen. She gave up her queenship for a crying knight?"

I think he means to annoy me. "My point is Gwenivere saw compassion. Lancelot thought he had killed another knight in a jousting match. He couldn't stand it; he got down on his knees and prayed for the guy to live *and he cried*. Compassion is a very attractive quality, Super Sup.

"And those two winding up together isn't such a stretch. His life was lonely, and he's a kind man who likes the role of rescuer. It doesn't hurt that he looks like Sir Lancelot, either. And she, in spite of the predicament she's in, is very attracted to compassion, to kindness. It's not a weakness to her. So you see, it's a Camelot story."

But the sup isn't interested in *Camelot*. "You're not on duty today. How come you're wearing your uniform?"

"I'm invited to this wedding, and they asked me to wear my uniform. Thought the guests might like that."

"That's against regulations."

It is such a happy occasion. Why can't he just flow with it?

"But the uniform is good for public relations. Anyway, I've been thinking of other things at the moment, like the dog whisperer struggling with fear of the dark, and the summer girl suffering rejection, the man in the straw hat and . . ."

He shakes his head, interrupts, "Why the hell do you keep avoiding people's names?" and leans forward, closer to my face. His expression is penetrating, the look, *the mask*. He goes on, "You put a tree in The Legacy Forest in memory of Dave Cato, but you're still calling him the man in the Panama hat. Doesn't the dog whisperer—he's the groom—have a real name? And the Marine who was killed. You still call him the menace? Will I always be the sup?"

"Super sup? The swaggering super sup of sleepy hollow. Oh, no, that's another story."

Refusing to be deflected, he persists, "And what would be the title of your story, Billie?"

I'm listening but aware that the wedding photography is nearly complete.

"They're waving you over, Billie," he observes.

"Uh-oh. They want the baby in some of the pictures and she's asleep." I get up and move away, but still my sup persists.

"What would be your title, Billie? Don't evade."

"I don't know. Did you see *Dances with Wolves*?"

"Movies again?"

"Yes. His name was John Dunbar but the Indians renamed him Dances with Wolves cause that was his story. His love interest was Stands with a Fist . . ."

"This is Fox Brook Park in Brookfield, Wisconsin, in the 21st century. We have names."

"Our names used to tell our stories. Like if you were Jacobson, you were the son of Jacob. Or if you're John

Baker, you probably had an ancestor who was a baker or if you were Bakersfield . . ."

"Earth to ranger, Earth to ranger," he mocks.

But the sup is interrupted by an interloper, an adolescent wedding guest who shouts, "What if there were a guy in the park named Dick Little!"

I watch the kid run away; simultaneously then the sup throws his head back and lets out one loud guffaw that turns heads including the baby's. I have never seen him laugh; he snorts when he laughs. It's a hee-haw thing. Now Allie's awake and whimpering, looking for the source of what must have seemed like an explosion. Her gaze is fixed on the cavernous open and bellowing mouth of the sup. She reaches toward him with little hands opening and closing as though she wants to touch his gold-capped molars or grasp the shiny sheriff badge on his shirt pocket. In either case her pixie laughter tinkles in the air. The sup, completely disarmed, bends down close to her face, lets her touch his badge and says, "And what would your name be? Talks with little fists? Laughs with little bells?" *He's human!*

And he's is on my wavelength now. "Okay, they all have real names, I know, but to me their names aren't as important as their stories. The stories are everything! People used to think the saddest thing for me during my mother's Alzheimer's was her forgetting my name. No. It was when she forgot not only *her* own name, but when she forgot who *she* was. She actually forgot her own history. She didn't know her own story. You lose those stories and you have lost yourself . . . I'm going to have to go, I think . . . ," but I lean toward the sup and lower my voice, "I used to be angry about everything like the menace was, not any more. Maybe I should call him the cure instead of the menace."

"Jesus Christ, I don't know."

"Stop swearing in front of the baby. She can hear, you know. I have to go!"

He shifts his attention to the baby, addresses her, "I'm not swearing. I'm summoning help," then back to me, "Wait. Are you coming back next season? You like it here, don't you?"

"Yes. Very much. But I don't know if I'm coming back … and right now I need to be on my way to the wedding group at the front of the chapel to deposit my charge." I don't answer the question, *are you coming back?*

Undeterred, he calls after me, "You should come back. You have to come back because *your* story isn't finished."

I have to turn around at that. I tell him, "My story here might be finished now."

"Because of this wedding?'

"No. Because of the letter."

. . . .

CHAPTER 15

LETTER FROM HOG: HUNTER OF GUNS

I'll be damned. A letter from a Fox Brook ranger. Ranger Billie, I can't quite picture you; I met more than a few rangers at Fox Brook, none that I made any effort to remember. Cause of my pretty bad reputation

there, I'm surprised to get such a cordial letter. Brookfield, my past there, kind of a blur.

When I think of Fox Brook Park, I see just animation. A fairy tale. Myself in a cartoon. Maybe a little guerilla pacman, running around hiding, but in absolutely no danger. Looking for trouble where I almost had to work hard to find some.

Skip all that; my real life started when I joined the Marines. My instructor in sniper school talked like this: subversive nature, ability to disappear, not be captured or intimidated, dispassion for the enemy—all strengths for an operative who acts alone. If that sounds like out of a textbook, it's because it is out of a textbook. It's academic training, and just so you know, there are no stupid snipers. I excelled in physical training, too. Me now: Primarily a hunter who lives in the shadows. Professional killer living behind my scope, when I have a target. Are you surprised?

Even though we're embedded with the ANA [Afghan National Army], insurgents really are after the ETT [Embedded Training Team]—that's us. They want to take us out. They have snipers, too. Anyway, what we do most of the time is wait. Insurgents keep coming back at us, and we keep killing them. They keep coming, they stop for a while. They study us. They wait and we wait. Then they move or we move and then wait some more. I like to be moving but that's when we're most vulnerable.

We think they pay villagers to alert them when we're coming. Like we see puffs of smoke coming out of chimneys all of a sudden as we approach a village, or someone sets a bunch of pigeons loose, or dogs bark or car horns start blaring. And they watch to see what we do when we're fired on, where we hide or run to. Then they put I.E.D.s there. They just watch, take their time, pretty cunning, not backward at all when it comes to fighting.

Anyway, Ranger Billie, you think you have problems? How about this? I've seen guys die, both the enemy and also one of my own team. That's right, snipers don't work solitary all the time. And when you lose someone on your team, you wonder if he'd still be alive if you had done something differently. You doubt yourself. I mean the worst thing is to let your buddy down.

My partner and I worked as a team. I had my target sighted, waited for his head to come out from behind a concrete pillar. The idea was a head shot when he looked out. My partner was supposed to back me up. But the plan didn't work. I don't know where my target came out, how he got the opportunity for the shot, but he dropped my partner. I had my sight set on where I thought the target was, but I heard the shot, heard my partner crumple, and then I saw the bastard target cut and run in the other direction. I aimed for the waist/hip section of his body, where there's a mass of bone and gut, and I knew I'd drop him. He would bleed to death, or I might finish him off later, but he's not taking any of us out, so I got the job done. Only problem is, he's already taken out my partner.

I wonder what I missed, if I blinked when my target moved or whatever. What I could have done better, could I have saved him. Could I have kept him alive. You've probably heard of semper fidelis, "always faithful"? That means to the mission, to the corps, and to each other. You trust each other, especially in times of need (which is all the time over here), and you get unbelievably close in times of death.

That's what I was thinking about after I read your letter, the part about how your mother kept falling through the cracks, how you couldn't stop it, about the bad dreams. Yeah, I get all that.

Everybody here in my squad has been baptized back at home except me. If I get killed here, I want to go where the other guys are going. I told this to the chaplain, and he said he would baptize me right here in a little rivulet from the Helmand River that passes through our compound. It didn't matter if it wasn't the Jordan River or something Biblical; it would still take. So that's what he did, with my squad all around, and I felt better just about at that instant, knowing Jesus and knowing I could die.

When you read newspaper articles about the conflict over here or you see news photos or movies with Marines on point, scoping a target, what you can't see is they're praying, too. My buddies tell me I'm even more dangerous, more lethal now cause I'm a religious sniper. Well, okay, but I don't know if that's going to keep me alive.

My chaplain told me Jesus would forgive my sins and that I should forgive myself, too, and that's why I'm at peace here, of all places, with all the killing going on.

So, Ranger Billie, I'm writing back to you not cause I give a shit about the Micargi. The Micargi was nothing, just a toy. If you had stolen my ACOG [advanced optical gunsight], 4 powered, and my M40A1 sniper rifle, I'd kill over that. (See I belong here; you should stay in Fox Brook Park.)

I'm writing to you to ask you to pray for me and to promise that I'll pray for you. (You can count on me.)

And my advice to you is, for whatever you think you didn't do right, forgive yourself.

. . . .

And I finally did.

CHAPTER 16

GOING, GOING, GONE . . .

. . . .

LOG ENTRY

Date: *Oct. 24*

Closing time: 10 p.m. Park is secure. Ranger not needed here. That's my story and I'm sticking to it.

10-42

. . . .

My last log entry, last of the season, last . . . period, more like a conclusion. I radio my supervisor, for the last time. "This is 935 to 930, requesting 10-42."

"10-4," my sup answers.

That's it? So professional, so generic, so detached.

My cell phone rings, and I anticipate the sup making a cordial, maybe even personal, farewell.

"Hi, Sup."

"Hi, Billie. Did you see Merwin yet?" The sup always referred to him accurately, by his real name.

"What? No, not tonight. Haven't seen him in a while. Why?"

"He was in the park this morning, asking about your schedule. He was afraid he missed you."

"Does he want to say good bye?" *Do you want to say goodbye?*

"I don't know. Said he wanted to talk to you *in person* and that he'd be back tonight to catch you before you left. He doesn't do anything that isn't important to someone, so I'm surprised he didn't follow through. He seemed kind of harried, though."

"Well, no see'um. So are *you* going to say good bye?" I finally ask.

"Nope, not goodbye. I'm going to say happy trails and sweet dreams until we meet again."

"I didn't hang up my spurs, but I left my uniform for good and turned in my badge. Now I'm hearing a song about the tumbling tumbleweeds, and I'm having a vision of John Wayne."

"That really dates you, Billie, but it sure beats the rants of your first season."

"I'm kind of embarrassed even remembering those days, those *dark* days."

"Well, you came for a distraction, remember? You came to escape."

"Yes, Merlin would say, 'to relieve suffering.' It did help."

"Did the Marine ever find out that you were the one who trashed his bike?"

I never told anyone about the bike and now I'm talking with an officer of the law, a former sheriff's deputy, my supervisor. And *he knows.*

"You know," he continues, "I spent my adult life going after criminals, examining crime scenes, noting clues . . . reading people."

"So what clue gave me away?"

"When the crying boy who knocked you off the boardwalk confessed, remember I was there, I was watching you. It was written all over your face."

"That I'm a criminal?"

"No. That you were feeling guilty. And, no, you're not a criminal. Criminals don't look guilty because they don't feel guilty. They look mad, cause they got caught. Anyway, former Ranger Billie, we helped you find your way," followed by a brusque, "Now put in a good word for the park system. 10-4." Just a click and he is gone.

....

I take a last look at the dark dumpster, site of many raccoon skirmishes, the picnic bench of countless lunches and the pile of contraband that was the Marine's Fox Brook secret, the Silverado, my mechanical workhorse, anathema to the sensibilities of the Lexus-driving Queen of Sheba, and the thought of that woman makes me smile now . . . *I was in pain and I thought she couldn't feel any, too insulated . . . too wealthy . . . probably could buy the nursing home Dave Cato put his wife in . . . now I don't have any feelings about her one way or the other.*

On to my Toyota. The lot is all shadow and I never liked this part—walking from the darkened park office to my car. Where's Merlin? If he's is going to make an appearance, now is the time because I'm driving away, looking west where I've locked up the beach house for the last time, there's the flag flying at full staff—no one from Wisconsin killed in Afghanistan today, illumination that looks like UFOs . . . *What?*

Beneath the lot lamp, dreamlike shining rays highlight white hair and a white beard, a spectral Santa Clause or a surreal magician. *Right out of the woods, right out of Camelot. Yup. It's Merlin.*

I approach the hazy park exit and roll down my window for a better view of Merlin's face. His features are sunken, cadaverous in bizarre shadows from overhead lighting. He says, "I didn't want to creep out of the darkness and scare you."

"You look kind of ghostly under the lamp light, though. Did you know today's my last day here?"

"I haven't been in the park lately, except this morning. Someone told me you were leaving, and then I thought about what I did and it started to bother me."

"You did something wrong? I thought you were Ghandi practically!"

"No, Ghandi was Hindu and I'm not. And, no, it wasn't wrong. I just didn't imagine what might happen."

"Now I'm pretty curious and mainly because you chose me to tell."

"I thought you'd understand and . . . help."

"Oh, man. Why don't you get inside my car, Merlin, and sit down. You look tired." Merlin's leaning against the light pole like he can't sustain his own weight.

"No, I'll just stay out here." He reaches into his pocket and places the contents into the worn palm of his right hand, then proffers it to me.

"That's a ring; is it a class ring?"

"Uh huh."

"Well, well. You found another one! Couldn't you find the owner?"

"I know who it belongs to. It belongs to the Marine."

Then he told his tale, how he saw the class ring among the Marine's buried possessions, how he thought the Marine would feel bad to come back from war and find out his ring was impounded by the sheriff's department, how the last thing that should happen to his ring is "them law enforcement folks take ownership of it."

"So I took it," he says. "I intended to wait 'til he got back from his deployment and then give it to him myself."

"And get about the biggest thank you ever!"

"Yes. See why I told you? I knew you'd get it."

"Now what are you going to do, give it to his parents? They're divorced now. You'd have to pick one or the other."

"That's not what I was thinking. I was thinking of giving it to you to give to that little girl, Alice, well, Allie, when she gets older. Don't give it to her now cause she might swallow it and choke."

"Why don't *you* give it to her when she's a little older, Merlin? She would give you one sweet thank you, I bet."

"Look at me, Ranger Billie . . ."

"Just Billie now," I correct him.

"Look how old I am. My bus is about ready to leave. By the time she's a little older, I might be a little dead."

"Oh, for Pete's sake."

Merlin persists, "Now you take it, and if you do this for me, I'll save you a seat on that bus. And I'll ask the driver to return when it's time to punch your ticket."

Then he plunges a closed fist through the open window, past my face, and releases his grip. The ring bounces from passenger side to the floor beneath my seat. I scramble awkwardly, fumble under my seat, feel the ring, clamp my fingers around it, jerk upward trying to right myself, the back of my head slamming into the steering wheel . . . I think, actually feel . . . a searing wave of pain behind my closed eyes . . . a tempest of energy . . . *like the time in third grade, I stuck a wire into an electrical socket with one hand while my other hand held the other end of the wire and a light bulb . . . to see if the bulb would light and like a soul passed right through me . . . it hurts, it hurts . . . but it passed through, like through the valley of the shadow . . . he's gone, they're gone, but it's just the grief, just pain, so what . . . of course I'll give her the ring* . . . then regain my composure, my upright posture.

"I'll give it to her, Merlin. Of course . . . Merlin?"

I turn back to the open window and stare wide-eyed beyond the narrow slit of illumination beneath the street light.

Merlin is gone.

CHAPTER 17

ONE OF "THEM THANK-YOU LETTERS"

Dear Merlin,

I was walking civilian style in The Legacy Forest yesterday, half expecting to find a tree planted in your memory. Instead I ran into the Indian-walking ranger who trained me a few years ago. She said you didn't die, you didn't get on the metaphorical "bus." You took a real Greyhound bus to Florida after your brother, who lives in Miami, bought you a ticket for the umpteenth time and you finally went. Now you don't want to come back and I don't blame you. Talk about beaches to troll. And thank-you letters to read . . .

Here's mine.

I had the ring framed in a shadow box so Allie could have it hanging on a wall in her bedroom and not have to wait until she was old enough not to swallow it. Allie's mother says I should take it out of the box and give it to her when I'm ready and at the same time tell her about the menace of Fox Brook Park, about how he became a Marine and about how she came to be. I'm looking forward to explaining how we were all wrong, well, mainly me, wrong about her Marine father. He was struggling back then, suffering, you said, but he was fearless and selfless all bundled together into one angry and complicated package. We were all lucky to have known him.

So thank you for making me take the ring. Thanks for letting me do something for the Marine.

Merlin, thanks for your magic.

ACKNOWLEDGEMENTS

For their much appreciated contributions, I thank
Rick Harder, Liz Dixon, Beth Jensen, Kathy Clarey,
Rene Benson, Joan Randolph, Annette Harder
and the late Richie Schuppler.